STILL WATERS

ALSO BY MELANIE GREENE

Hearts of Honey Wine Series
Common Ground *(Livia & Greg)*
Still Waters *(Amalia & Dante)*
New Flames *(Maggie & Adrian)*

Dunway Siblings Series
Feather in Her Cap *(Jeannie & Brendan)*
Twelve Scorching Days *(Sarita & Scorch)*
Margo of the Bells *(Margo & Karl)*
Away With a Stranger *(Andi & Cole)*

Pier 3 Coffee Series
Mocha for Mateo *(Alicia & Mateo)*
Cappuccino for Callie *(Abraham & Callie)*
Latte for Leyla *(Austin & Leyla)*
Curiosity (Amity & Josh)
Polar Opposites *(Audra & Salt)*

Roll of the Dice Series
Rocket Man *(Serena & Dillon)*
Ready to Roll *(Janice & Miguel)*
Eye of the Tiger *(Natalie & Evan)*
Let the Good Times Roll *(Chloe & Gabriel)*
Roll of a Lifetime *(Rachel & Theo)*
Roll Play *(Kim-ly & Tómas)*
On a Roll *(Gillian & Vic)*
Roll in the Hay *(Anton & Cisco)*

STILL WATERS

MELANIE GREENE

Jennifer –
You are The Best
Thanks,
Melanie

Copyright © 2025 by Melanie Greene

All rights reserved.

This is a work of fiction, a product of the author's imagination, and any resemblance to real people or events is entirely coincidental. No part of this book may be reproduced in any form or by any electronic or mechanical means, including information storage and retrieval systems, without written permission from the author, except for the use of brief quotations in a book review. For information, contact Melanie Greene.

No Artificial Intelligence (AI) was used in the creation of this work. The author explicitly forbids the use of this work for training of all AI technologies, including those designed for the generation of text and images, and explicitly reserves all rights to license this work for any and all such uses in the future.

First edition: May 2025

Still Waters/by Melanie Greene

Cover Design by Melanie Greene

ISBN: 978-1-941967-52–2

For my truly superb parents, who taught me about welding and plumbing and art and love

CHAPTER 1

"Keep that focus on your breath. Let the weight of your hands pull your knee to your chest, and hold there. Think about the moment you're in now, not the moments you came from before entering this space."

Amalia Reyes's problem was, no matter how she centered and re-centered herself, her yoga teacher Sheila's instructions were only moving her muscles, not settling down her mind.

Next time, she wouldn't do anything as infuriating as stopping by to visit Mike Moll on her way to yoga. But she'd created a schedule for herself, to keep accountable to her goals, and that meant it was once again time to approach him with her portfolio. She could have put it off a day or two, but she'd finished her other admin work early, and his art gallery was right around the corner from the yoga studio.

So she went in, polite professional smile in place, offered a civil greeting to Mike's assistant, waited on his condescending to make time for her. The place was, as usual, a bit overfull of the same sorts of things. A pastiche mashup of fin de siècle and Texana that, presumably, sold well, even if it didn't reflect the full range of local artistic traditions, like Mike claimed.

Amalia hadn't gone in expecting Mike Moll to budge in

his views. She wasn't that kind of fool, not with the way Mike liked doubling down on being sure he knew better than anyone what art buyers wanted. And maybe he did, maybe he could stock Amalia's work year-round and not sell a single sculpture, but she still wanted to wedge her way into the town's annual festival. And that, unfortunately, meant dealing with Mike.

It didn't help now that, as she moved into Cobra pose, there was Dante Morales right in front of her, stripped to his little shorts, back muscles glistening in the heated studio. Normally, he was a pretty distraction from whatever thoughts tried to intrude during their hot yoga class. Nothing put her in the moment like tracing the ways his long limbs stretched and flexed in front of her. Maybe it was rude of her, to enjoy his objectively nice form, when she wasn't interested in anything beyond casual friendship from him, but: it was a good form. And his quietly solid presence in their social group hadn't changed, back when she'd turned down his offer to take her out. He'd accepted her statement about not looking for a relationship and still turned up to yoga every week. So maybe he wasn't interested in how she viewed him.

But Dante had been there that afternoon, at Moll's on Main. Doing some sort of something she hadn't been aware of, until he emerged from the back room with his tool belt low on his lean hips, just in time to hear Mike disparage her talent, her value, and her place in the Honey Wine art scene.

Again.

The way those brown eyes of Dante's had lingered on her as he stood behind Mike, listening in on the gallery owner's judgment of everything she'd ever done with her career. As it turned out, she was invested in how her friends viewed her. It was somehow more unbearable to receive Mike's judgments with Dante lurking nearby.

And then Dante had clanged his toolbox on the counter and pulled out his phone, saying, "Sorry, I can't get to this today. Looks like I could schedule you ... a week from Tuesday. Four p.m.?"

Then he just stood there while Mike protested and grumbled. He rolled one strong shoulder back in a mild shrug when Mike threatened to call a competitor.

And then, when she'd caught him waiting outside to walk with her to Shelia's studio, he'd said, "I could have finished the sink in three minutes, but Mike's bullshit distracted me into putting the bad coupling nut back in place."

It was infuriatingly nice, and Amalia did not appreciate his quiet show of sympathy. Her career was her own to deal with; no one needed to put their own business at risk because Mike Moll was kind of a jerk.

So ogling Dante didn't ground her in class in the least. The flex of his ass as they all moved only sent another wave of irritation through her. Amalia dropped her head towards the mat and focused on maintaining equal weight on her limbs, letting the energy move to her core with her breath, and imagining her negativity sweating out through her pores.

She'd expected the rejection from Mike. He'd never once given her portfolio serious consideration. He paid no attention to her sales numbers, or to her facts about the true origins of Honey Wine. His mother had been more receptive, back before she retired and left the place in his hands. She'd stocked a decent amount of Amalia's early sculpture, given her one of the earliest breaks into her career as a sheet metal sculptor. Mike, however, was determined to believe that work arising from the white Bohemians who settled in Honey Wine in the mid-1800s fully represented the cultural and artistic traditions of the town.

Enough. She settled herself into a twist and idly scanned the room for sights that didn't drag her thoughts into her problems. A community of dimly lit dripping bodies; the fading mandala mural above the mirrors; Sheila's pastel peace sign headband. Her shoulder blades dropped as she breathed in. Her spine obliged by giving a bit more as she let the breath go.

As the class sank into Savasana, Amalia's breath was a smooth glide from nose to throat to lungs to belly. Her arms and legs sank into the mat. Behind her eyes, a succession of colors wove sinuously together. She came back to herself as she breathed in Sheila's mist of mint and eucalyptus, letting the slightly astringent tang bring her mind back to the studio.

She reached for her hand towel and wiped down her face and chest. The couple beside her silently offered to take her blocks to be cleaned and returned. She smiled her thanks and moved to the wall to roll and stash her mat in its carrier and finish off her water bottle. She was heading to get a refill when Dante Morales, most recent witness of her professional disrespect, placed himself in her way.

※※※♥※※※

Two minutes after finishing their hot yoga class was not the right time to ask Amalia for sex lessons.

Somehow, it's still what Dante did.

He'd been thinking about it for days, and somehow, breaking the ice with her before yoga had been the spur prodding him to open his damn mouth.

"Amalia?"

She spun to face him, face bright with sweat and ... just bright. Amalia Reyes was a bright light of a person, always poised to fly off in whatever direction she aimed for. Quick and sure and never at a loss.

Dante often found himself at a loss. He drew in a deep breath, settling his post-workout heart into a calmer rhythm. Let it out gently as he tipped his chin down, speaking more directly to her. "I have a favor to ask."

"Sure. You need a ride?" She wrapped her towel around

her neck, nodding. "No, you had you van at Mike's. What's up?"

He pictured her riding him. His grasping the ends of the towel, to pull her down for a kiss. Their sweat-slick bodies sliding together.

Tried not to calculate the odds that she'd only sweat when she was with him because of working out. That he'd be useless at inspiring any slickness from her most intimate places. That he wouldn't bring anything to the encounter to elevate her heart rate.

Dante swallowed hard and shifted his mat. Contemplating his lackluster skills was always depressing, but at least he wasn't flashing a stirring dick to their whole yoga studio. "Thanks. It's, yeah, it's more personal. Can I get a few minutes? Buy you a smoothie?"

At the cafe beside their gym, he scoped out the nearby people. The way Honey Wine worked, he expected nosy locals everywhere he went. The place was, for the moment, clear of anyone he knew he'd have to face later.

Only Amalia. But when he'd thought through what he was going to do about his biggest problem, he knew he'd have to tell her just about everything. It was going to suck, and no amount of practice got him to the point of figuring out how to express himself with any ease. Which was probably part of his problem, at least according to the internet. What the internet wasn't good for, it turned out, was letting him solve the problem on his own.

He needed a helper. And Amalia was ... well, she wasn't nice, but she was true. Dante gravitated towards people who were true. He felt like whatever happened with his big ask, he could trust her.

After picking up their drinks, he made his way to the cafe table where she waited with their workout gear. She was looking strong, and vibrant, and open in a way that let him sit down across from her and spit it out.

Dante said, "I'm looking for someone who can teach me how to fuck."

⇢⇢⟫⟫♥⟪⟪⇠⇠

Amalia was grateful that the sweaty backs of her thigh stuck her to the padded vinyl chair, because otherwise she might have fallen over. She'd been thinking he'd ask for a positive job review, or a reference letter for some cousin trying to break into the art scene. Maybe even that he wanted to squeeze his six foot plus frame onto her ordinary little sofa while his place was under repair.

She was a woman of great imagination, but Dante's actual question never would have occurred to her.

She slurped her smoothie hard enough to give herself brain freeze, which didn't help her come up with anything to say, except, "Okay, but I know you're not a virgin."

Dante's head dropped so hard to the table that when he finally looked back at her, his forehead bore the imprint of the mesh tabletop. "Great. Go on. Tell me what you've heard."

"No, come on, you know I escape gossip from everyone but my family. But didn't you live with Elizabeth, back before she moved? You can't tell me that was a celibate arrangement. And you dated Shawna for a good while, back in the spring."

At the mention of his exes, Dante slumped as if they hadn't just spent an hour strengthening their cores. He got real focused on chasing a chunk of fruit around the bottom of his cup with his straw. She waited him out. He finally stopped examining the substrate of his drink and glanced at her. "That's it?"

"Is there some scandal I haven't heard about?"

His chest hitched. "Crap, no. No, that's not the gossip. Elizabeth only moved in for a month when her landlord wouldn't extend her lease before she took off for that Chicago job. I don't … there's no scandals, okay?"

She'd never seen him all flustered. He was redder than after an hour in the hundred degree workout studio. Amalia raised her eyebrows at him. "Chill. I wasn't suggesting anything dramatic. Just trying to figure out why you're asking ... whatever it is that you're asking. Which, to be clear, I still don't know. Is this a theory thing, or practical help?"

Dante rubbed his face, then crossed his arms. Tensed then relaxed his jaw. Blew out a breath. Met her eyes. "Okay, so I guess I knew this would be embarrassing, but. I've come this far. And you can walk away whenever you want this conversation to end. So. Thing is, I found out there are rumors about me. And since I'm not the most successful at hanging on to partners, I guess there's no reason for me to doubt them. I'm sure my cousins will be happy to share the worst of the details, but what it boils down to is that I'm ... apparently anyway, I'm pretty bad at sex. And relationships, but maybe that's because of the bad sex?"

Amalia found herself fascinated with the process of stirring her own smoothie to a uniform consistency. Dante reverted to form, not speaking at all, not even when she flat out asked, "Okay, but why?"

She meant a lot of things.

Why her? Why did he need this favor? Why bring it to her and not, say, some Reddit forum? Surely there was porn just for this, and books? While it wasn't her area of art history, she knew there'd been sex how-to guides written across civilizations and centuries. Back in December, she'd overheard a group in the diner laughing about how one of them had been accidentally given a copy of *Cosmopolitan Karma Sutra*, instead of the history of transatlantic shipping the giver had meant to wrap for that particular person. So it couldn't be that difficult for Dante to learn whatever he needed to learn.

Which was another *why*? Why did he even need this? He had, they'd agreed, the ability to successfully find people to date. Not that she'd made a point of noticing the occasional women who showed up with him at bars or dinner parties. Or on the mat beside his at yoga, looking like they were specifically designed to tuck under Dante's long arms as they wandered the Town Square together.

And if he could ask Amalia, surely he could also have asked one of them. Any of them. Either before, during, or after, the times they went to bed together.

She wasn't any kind of therapist, or teacher, or sex expert. And it didn't seem like this was a roundabout way of him asking her out again. He was too flat-out flustered for it to be a pick-up angle, even if he'd been the kind of guy who'd try such a bullshit line. Which he wasn't, not from what she knew after them moving in the same basic circles since he'd gotten grown enough to hang with their hometown crowd.

Maybe she didn't know him like she thought; maybe Dante was one of those guys who wanted to take possession of her time and energy and mental load. It fuddled her up, a confusion made worse by his downcast eyes and pouty lips, just a touch damp after releasing his straw. And by his ongoing silence.

Just before she gave up on an answer and walked out, he set aside his cup and said, "I wasn't ever, you know, assertive about figuring it all out with anyone. And then I was awkward and—you know, porn isn't good at teaching the logistics, not really. When I've asked Shawna or anyone, it … it didn't work right, asking them how. Not if they already knew I was no good. Put me too in my head, maybe. Wasn't their fault. So I figure I need to learn from someone I'm not dating, not trying to make the person I might marry someday."

She wasn't prepared for the foolish impulse to empathize, but damn if it didn't happen anyway. Probably that scene at Mike's, when Dante stood in silent defense of her, went and made her heart want to be supportive of him in return. Her voice came out almost gentle. "And that's me?"

He took her empty cup and tossed their trash, cause apparently he'd do anything to not keep eye contact. "You're a friend, and you're always honest. And you didn't want to date me, that time when I asked. Look, Amalia, I know it's my problem, and probably not worth your efforts. I don't know even how exactly you'd fix me, if you do agree to help, but I know I can count on you to not make the gossip worse. I trust you to tell me no. Either now, or after we talk about it more, or even if we get started and you want to end it. So. Yeah. If you're up for it, I'd like it to be you."

He was poised to escape, but hovering like some part of him hoped against hope for her agreement.

She closed her eyes while she called to mind her schedule. He stilled when she nodded, and followed her out the door. "Let me think it through a bit. Come over on Saturday and we'll talk."

CHAPTER 2

When Dante arrived to a job site, he usually took a few minutes to look over the call sheet, and double-check client notes, and log his start time. Grab a snack or drink from his cooler, if the time was right. Check he didn't have food in his teeth. Do box breathing, sometimes, to get focused on the work.

Whether he was in his customized cargo van full of all he'd need for most plumbing jobs, or the cab of the pick-up he used for personal transport and to dispatch his apprentice on small jobs and errands, he was always at ease behind the wheel. Comfortable and prepared for whatnot was next.

So the jumpy way he felt as he put the truck in park outside Amalia's place on Saturday afternoon, he didn't like that. He didn't like the skittering under his skin, or how he kept shifting around as if his driver's seat wasn't practically molded to his exact shape. Didn't like his clenched jaw.

She'd agreed to talk it out. Maybe even to help him. He'd counted on figuring out who to ask being the worst part of realizing he wasn't managing to fix things by himself. He was seeking someone reliable, someone smart, someone he liked. Someone discreet, if possible. He'd ruminated for a few days, moving through his life. Work, working out, gatherings, the bar. His first pick was Amalia Reyes, but he let himself stew on the problem until he was certain. And until he had the wherewithal to approach her.

Having accomplished that much, he'd hoped accepting her invite to discuss it in private would feel safe. Maybe even easy.

He'd hoped wrong.

Dante gave himself one glance in the mirror to all-clear his looks, and hauled himself out of the cab. Looked for solace in the familiar thud of the closing door, the habitual way he tucked his keys in the left front pocket of his jeans. Didn't let himself back out when none of that comfort came around.

She was right there as he mounted her porch. Door open before he'd finished wiping his shoes. He looked up to find her leaning against the interior hallway, leggings and tank like she often wore to yoga. Barefoot, too, which he'd also seen at the studio, but which struck him different, somehow, at the entrance to her home.

"Hey, Dante."

Probably he'd been staring. He looked down again, checked his soles were okay before crossing her threshold and handing over the potted lavender he'd brought her. "Hi. Thanks for having me."

She led him into a sitting room. Her house was concrete floors and overlapping rugs and more colors than a sunset in fire season. Dante was in and out of peoples' homes all the time, and didn't tend to take much notice of the decor or how it reflected whoever lived there. Amalia's choices, though, he noticed.

Maybe because she invited him to sit, when usually he was passing through to wherever the plumbing problem waited for him. Maybe because she was an artist, and it made him see all the ways she'd brought beauty and interest to the place. Hanging plants and different kinds of chairs and a level row of tiny oval paintings mounted between the windows.

Whatever the reason, Dante noticed, and kept noticing. Every time he moved on from cataloging one element, another one caught his eye.

"Do you want a drink?"

He stopped himself from staring around and looked at his host. His friend—maybe, he hoped, even a good friend.

Even more hopefully, the person whose help he'd soon earn. "Sorry. Yeah. Anything's good."

"Beer?"

"Whatever you're having."

She gave him a look like he wasn't following the script. Like he needed to catch up with how she was prompting him along. "I might have rotten taste in drinks."

Okay, banter. He could remember how to banter. "Is it worse than pickle juice in soda? Cause I tried that trend," he said. "You're making the face I'd expect, but it wasn't so bad."

Now she was laughing. Dante knew he must have seen her laugh before, but maybe he'd never been the one to make it happen.

She had a good laugh. Robust. The chime of it lingered in her tone when she said, "I'll break out the Clamato and hot sauce, but you won't find pickles in my fridge."

He rose from the deep green chair he'd settled in and followed. It made things better, to move around the kitchen with her. To take down the pint glasses from what looked to be her highest shelf—chin level for him, and he didn't need the flash of her eyes to know he wasn't about to risk teasing her about their height difference.

One thing Dante knew as a deep truth was the bullshit that took up residence in your brain from even a minor comment about your appearance. Too much of his youth had involved overhearing other people's opinions about his apparently sub-par body.

So he handed over the glasses, and moved to scrub his hands before slicing the lime she'd set on a chopping board.

She gestured at a bag of tortilla chips. He dumped them into a bowl and put a smaller one beside it for the salsa she opened. She told him where to recycle the beer bottles, while she dug through some drawer for what turned out to be napkins.

It wasn't routine, but it was all familiar. Easy, as he set the snacks in front of her and tucked away her intel about the potter who'd made the bowls, for when he was Mother's Day shopping. He felt settled into his stance, and barely rocked back at all when Amalia said, "So, I've been thinking about it, and before I can say if I'd be any help—can you try to explain what it is about fucking that you're doing wrong?"

※※※♥※※※

It wasn't her plan to take him unawares, but the look on his face suggested she'd thrown him. They'd said he was coming over to talk through this whole thing, and what did he think that meant? She could forgive the nerves she'd sensed when he arrived, but he'd seemed past them.

Amalia waited out Dante's intent wiping down of her kitchen counter. She didn't see any of the crumbs he was so intent on corralling into his cupped palm, but sure. Let him chase down any speck of tortilla chips that escaped confinement in her chip bowl, if it soothed him in some way.

"Hey, I get it's awkward—we all have our cultural baggage about what things are taboo to discuss openly—but this scheme is your idea. I'm curious to know more, to know what you want out of it. And if we're going to make any progress, we have to communicate, and what you're doing now, instead, is clamming up."

With a snap like an off-cut dropping to the shop floor, he sank into the kitchen stool beside hers and said, "Okay."

Just that. As if it answered every one of those awkward questions.

Amalia sipped her michelada. It was almost funny,

watching his slow-motion fidgeting. Tapping his fingers, but only one every two or three seconds. Shifting his weight half a limb at a time. When he finally faced her, he said, "Going back probably too far, but I was behind you, so maybe you don't remember. In school, I was never good at social stuff. They called me the tag-along. I hung out with the guys, but not to party or talk up girls. After that, apprenticing, I was the new kid. Younger, single when the other plumbers mostly had families already. I met some good people at union meetings, but it's always about work with them. My cousins are either a decade older than me or, what's worse, four-five years younger. They're the ones that told me I have a bad reputation."

She couldn't help snorting. "Little Leo is the one prompting all this? That kid doesn't know how not to give shit to everyone he meets."

Dante's head tilted a few degrees to the left. It somehow made that crooked incisor of his just a tad too cute when he next spoke. "Nah, I'd have ignored it if it was just Leo. But then last month, Enrique came at me, too."

She winced a little; though Enrique was barely out of college, he somehow had all the gravitas his brother missed out on. Amalia didn't have time for Leo's consistent goofballness, but Enrique was like the mini-mayor of Honey Wine. "Right, yeah, that's a different matter. Okay, then, for whatever reasons, you didn't learn to hang out easily, and, what? It stopped you from learning how to kiss?"

He dropped his gaze to his restless hands again. "I know I need to say all of this. I came over to be honest, and I know that means telling you things that—that show my faults. If you want to hear me out, still. I trust you, even if I'm awkward at expressing myself. Even if you're going to know all my worst stuff, I trust you."

She took a beat to absorb all that. She'd never been in this situation, being handed someone's vulnerabilities without any kind of lead-up. It was intense. Flattering, in a way, to be the one he'd picked, even if it had already turned intrusive. Not the moments hanging out talking over drinks—those were normal as anything. But the way this fucking request kept slipping into her thoughts when she was meant to be otherwise occupied. That wasn't in her conquer things timeline.

"Worst stuff, huh?"

"Did that sound ominous? Shit. There's nothing creepy, I don't think."

"You don't think so. Great."

He clearly picked up her sarcasm, and shrugged into a half-smile. "I just meant I never had that youthful exploration phase. I got in a loop of hanging back, not asking for what I wanted. Girls were okay being friends, but by the time I thought about more, they'd moved on. So I fell behind everyone else—or what I was convinced everyone else was up to, at least."

"And that's what you're worried about? Not enough experience thanks to being an awkward teenager? Aren't you a grown man now?"

He sucked air like his lungs were just learning to work. "I am. I'll be thirty this year. I'm no incel, and I try not to be an asshole. I'm not blaming anyone for rejecting me back in high school. You know I date. I even dated back before I hit a growth spurt and the weight went into my height."

"So you are aware you did the ugly duckling to swan transformation thing." She'd paid little attention to him for a few years there, between summer day camp when he was the quiet, loner kid intent on following each step of the art projects she assigned her group, and then in their twenties when he was suddenly being handsome on the fringes of her friend group.

He gave her back her own dry tone. "I have a mirror, Amalia."

"Good. Then the beard is a choice and not because you can't see to shave it."

He laughed, which she'd intended. They both knew his beard was tidy. And attractive.

"Look, I think I'm off track. The why of how I came late to dating, to having a social life, I do think it had an impact on me. But, yeah. Late bloomer or not, I've had sex. My issue is," he paused. Rubbed his palms over his thighs. "I'm not satisfying my partners. I've tried asking them. I've tried looking stuff up, watching stuff. And—according to the intel Leo's telling me about—it's no good. So I thought if I could figure things out by talking to someone I trust, it might give me. I don't know. The kind of base line I need, if that makes sense, for a woman to believe I'm capable of pleasing her. Of making myself worth her time."

She traced a spiral in the condensation of her glass. "So this is your fix-it plan? Talk it through with someone, outside a romantic context?"

"Yeah. With you, if you will," he said. "I want to fall in love, but I can't be going into a life with someone always wondering what I'm doing wrong. Or listening to Leo and Enrique go out of their way to tell me for sure I'm doing wrong by her."

"I know they can be pests, but what is their deal? Are your exes really telling Leo intimate stuff about you?"

"Yeah? Or, at least in one case, and then he made an investigation out of it. Talked to roommates, friends, whoever they can find to say how I'm boring or awkward or that I put my hands in the wrong places. Enrique said women across the county are warning each other about me. That I may as well be a mannequin cause I'm nice to look at but don't know how to move right. And the more they repeat it, the more nervous I get, so I end up rigid as hell."

She could believe it, given how he'd turned to concrete on her bar stool. His eyes were fixed on the sunset through the window over the sink as he went on. "The last couple of dates were a bust, and Leo sought them out for more ammo, and now he and Enrique are making sure everyone knows I'm not worth putting up with."

"Why are they being such asses, though?" What she meant was more like, why didn't Dante shut that shit down, but he'd never been a shut shit down kind of guy.

Stiffly, he rolled his shoulders. "History. I mean, it blew up into this flood of bullshit last month after Leo caught wind of —well, he knows someone I dated, overheard her laughing with someone, picked it up and dragged his very willing brother along to dig up what they could. But also, back when I was with Elizabeth … so, they were only seventeen, eighteen at the time. And she said something they interpreted as me not being that smooth in bed. Which maybe she meant, but I don't think she intended them to hear her and start howling about it. I tried to snap back and it backfired. They got all puffed up, like I was poking at their own skills, and, well, young men's egos, you know?"

She snorted. She was a pretty young woman making a living as a sheet metal sculptor. She did, indeed, know men's egos.

CHAPTER 3

She propped an elbow on the counter and shook her head. "Okay. Cousins being jerks aside, I'll accept there's enough smoke to light this fire for you. So. Let's say we do this. What's in it for me?"

He examined Amalia's expression. She wasn't acting like she minded anything he'd let loose from his jumble of thoughts and worries. Or like he, in himself, was any kind of dealbreaker.

Which maybe meant it was a deal she was willing to make. If he could make it worthwhile. "Tell me anything you need. Any leaks to fix or drains you need snaked? Or, don't know if I told you, I'm certified now in water protection, so I can set up a rainwater irrigation system for you."

There he'd made her laugh again, but it was a sec before he understood why.

"Is this the start of an adult film?" She put on a low voice. "Lady, I'm the plumber, come to snake your drain."

"Ah, hell." He'd spent his whole adult life in the trade. It wasn't the first time he'd been in the midst of jokes about laying pipe.

"Hey lady, will you open my tool chest and grab me those nuts, so I can get to screwing?"

He waited. It wouldn't matter what he had to say, not while she was busy riffing about his profession.

"Let's see what we can do about this slow drip of yours. Maybe with a little suction we can get everything flowing just right."

Given how much of her art involved industrial equipment, he might ought to be surprised she hadn't brought up galvanized steel nipples, or clamps with deep jaws. Better to interrupt before she thought of anything on those lines. "I get it, you don't need my services. Professional services."

She bit her lips like it was a struggle not laughing at him. "I do want to know more about the irrigation, actually. I'm laying out a new section of my climate victory garden, hoping to get some fruit trees established this winter."

"Yeah?" He half-stood like he would inspect her yard, even in the dusk. "What's a climate victory garden?"

"A movement for people to address climate change by growing more of their own food, to reduce the problems with interstate and international transport. And the lack of diversity from single crop farming, the problems with pesticides, all that."

He tried, but Amalia didn't let him get sidetracked by anything as easy for him to discuss as her catchment area and plastic versus galvanized rain tanks.

"Listen, that's not what I had in mind. You heard all that Mike was saying at the gallery the other day, right?"

He nodded. He'd heard Mike's tone first, since his head was in the sink cabinet, and maybe would have ignored the snideness if Mike hadn't used it while saying Amalia's name. By the time he'd undid the fix he'd been in the midst of, packed up, and joined them, he'd also heard Mike say he knew her work was too 'multicultural' and also messy to fit in with his vision for what made tourists come to Honey Wine.

So he didn't regret getting pissy with Mike in return, even if Amalia had given him one of those perceptive looks that told him she'd never asked him to butt in. He suspected she'd been a little shook up about him overhearing all Mike's bullshit. When she brought it up herself, instead of assembling conversational barriers around it, it felt like trust.

"Yeah, is he always like that?"

"He can be. I expect it, but I need him right now. It's ... okay. Maybe you don't know also that Mike's Uncle Bill is also kind of old-school. I don't know how Mike's mom turned out to be so cool, honestly. But Bill, whenever I come into the hardware store, he's so damn condescending. I shop local businesses when I can, but that man vexes me with his insistence on sending his cashiers out to help load up my truck. The minute any woman buys more than ten pounds of anything from him, those literal children have to scramble to escort them to their cars. And if Bill treats me like some helpless little thing, and Mike doesn't take my art seriously, that means Jackson Apel doesn't even think of taking my side against them, no matter how much I thought he appreciates my work. From there, why would Frank Connor rock his organized boat of the way things have always been, and how, then, do I get him or anyone to listen to my proposal that Honey Wine should include the Mexican Americans who helped settle our town in this year's FoundersFest?"

She took a beat before continuing, and he focused in. Whatever Amalia had in mind to ask, he'd move every obstacle to fix it for her. Starting with Bill Moll, who'd always treated him like a favorite son, but now Dante would be alert to calling out his sexism and racism.

"So that's what I need. For someone those old-guard guys like a lot more than me, someone with some pull on the FoundersFest committee, to talk them into giving my proposal a fair hearing."

He didn't even blink. "I had no idea they were giving you trouble. I'm in."

"Now you know," she said. "So, yeah?"

"Absolutely, yeah. We'll give them hell."

※※※

Whether his fast acquiescence was due to being moved by her request, or his desperation for her to sort out his issues, she'd take it. As long as she wasn't getting herself into some unwinnable chore.

"Sweet. So, can we talk parameters? Now that I'm not taken aback by your ask in the first place, what are you envisioning? Cause your question was about fucking, and you're telling me more about your social history. I get how those can be intertwined, but which thing do you want help with? Or is it both?"

Dante swiveled a few degrees away, but that just put his shoulder in contact with hers. He startled a little, but didn't retreat. After a sec, she even felt him relax his weight more firmly against her side. He didn't look at her when he said, "Both."

"Do you want us to have actual sex?" It was a little abrupt, but she wasn't clear on how to get either of them to relax until they were talking more openly. It was why she'd asked him over, instead of trying to have the conversation somewhere anyone in their eternally nosy town might run across them.

He ran his hands over his face and muttered, "Well, not this minute."

"Dante, come on. I'm no good at sugar coating things, but what I'm trying to get at is understanding your needs, and your expectations. You said you tried asking dates, and the internet, and now we're here. I'm not suggesting we hop straight into bed, for the record."

"Good to know."

"Don't be a brat. We already said you're good-looking. But if you're bad at interpersonal stuff and at physical stuff—if there are women willing to talk to your cousins about that, maybe it's true—I don't think you can address one without the other. You know I'm not a couple-y person myself, but that doesn't mean I haven't seen how important it is for couples to bring the goods on both those fronts."

He sat straighter again, taking away all of those warm spots where they'd pressed together. His ears were red enough that she was sure he didn't need any of her body heat adding to his discomfort. It took him a couple of deep breaths before he got talking again. "That makes sense. Thanks. You're clever."

"Maybe. Maybe not. This isn't exactly something I've ever done, you know? But I think if you can handle me being honest with things—with feedback and boundaries and all—I can probably help at least a little. Just remember that I'm no expert, and also that you're allowed your own boundaries."

He was shaking his head. "No, Amalia, you're the one who makes the rules. I'm here begging for your help; it's up to you if you want to do anything physical, or to put a stop to everything, or what. I'll listen to you. I can handle it, like you asked."

She had all kinds of doubts, but not about him trampling across any boundaries. He sounded all too eager to throw himself into whatever lesson plan she came up with. "Okay, well. There's a couple of things I still want to know, but I feel like you're not having the easiest time talking about details."

"I can—"

"Relax. I want you to try something." Partly because his verbal fumbling wasn't giving her a consistent trail to follow about where his actual problems were. Partly because she remembered some advice from when she had to TA a couple of classes in college, and maybe it would come in handy again. "Get yourself a journal or notebook, and write out the stories of how you brought up being better at sex with women in the past. Not to identify them, nothing explicit; try to focus on the conversations, and your feelings, and outcomes. Don't try to draw any conclusions from it. Leave the conclusions until we can look at the stories together."

Dante took out his phone and typed out the assignment. "I'll give it a try. When do you want me to show you?"

She had to laugh a little. "You know, you're pretty agreeable. You sure your cousins aren't exaggerating to harass you?"

"They probably are, but. I can't keep asking women to put up with me on the chance I'll be okay. I have to be a decent partner in all the ways I can manage."

The man was on the verge of unraveling. He was still as could be, but she could sense some inner spring just desperate to pop up and send him spiraling.

She tapped the counter once, sharp. "So. You don't want to figure all this out from within a relationship?"

There went his breath, gusting again. "I … don't, no. I want …"

Nope. No more floundering. She didn't have time for him to flail and hide. "Dante, hey. You pulled up the nerve to ask me for help. No one else: me. Because you know I'll be honest, and discreet."

"Like I said."

"Don't be obstinate. I've got a suggestion, and I want you to think it over before you answer. You on board with that?"

His eyes fixed back on her. He nodded.

"I am guessing that what you want, Dante, is to be *good*. Good at romance, good in bed. Not a work in progress. And along with whatever else we're learning about each other, something I think might be true—but that you might not have articulated—is that in particular, you don't want a girlfriend who has to tell you *how* to become good. You want to come to someone confident in your skills, so you can offer up, I'm betting, both your heart and your body, as a ready-to-woo package. You want her to know from the outset that you'll be making every effort for the relationship. That your every effort will please her. What you want is for her to look at you and know she can ask you to grant her any kind of pleasure, and you'll have the willingness, and the skills, to make that happen."

He was glazed over again. Silent.

She suppressed her own desire to get lost imagining what that kind of relationship would feel like. After banking her own feelings, and judging he'd had time to absorb her idea, she asked, "Does what I'm suggesting sound at all correct?"

CHAPTER 4

"Um, yes," Dante nearly clapped his hand over his mouth. He wasn't somebody who blurted out answers, but when Amalia asked if what she said felt right, everything in him was eager to agree. She'd asked him to consider it before responding, but he didn't need time. It was nothing he'd thought about in the past, but it might be all that was on his mind for the future.

The way she grinned left him guessing that his ears had gone red. He sipped his drink, just for the chance to run a cool hand over the nape of his neck.

She tapped her fingers against his forearm and said, "Don't go dissolving into silence on me. I can't spend our whole time together reminding you that you have to communicate."

"No, yeah, I get that." Dante set his shoulders. "I won't let it be a problem."

When Amalia tapped his forearm again, it was with a fraction more pressure, and for a fraction more time. The band constricting his chest eased up. "So if I can wrangle the town council and Mike—I can't believe he's chair of the Art Walk again." He hadn't been paying too much attention to FoundersFest yet, other than setting up his usual sponsorship, but he knew Mike had wrangled a second appointment to chair the visual arts portion of things, even though he was supposed to rotate out of the role after two years.

Amalia hummed her agreement.

"So I'll get you in there, and then you'll help me out?"

Amalia licked her lips and gave him one of those up and down looks that prodded his cock to get ahead of reality. He was going to spend all his time horny and embarrassed until all this was over. He sipped, again, hoping to cool his whole face.

"I trust you, too, you know."

Her words perked him right up. "Yeah?"

"Yeah. So you say you'll help with Mike, and I trust that. I don't need you to check off some to-do list before I help you. We'll work together on both our needs."

He felt drunker than one beer merited. Dizzy not with worry that he couldn't help her out—it would push him into some difficult conversations, but her goals were more important than his discomfort—but with some kind of euphoria that he might get fixed, himself.

Amalia had every chance to refuse him, to disregard him, to let him live on with all his awkward and inept romance. But she'd listened, and seen right to the core of him.

She saw he needed to get romancing right for whoever he ended up with. He needed to start out able to give his partner pleasure. Needed her never having to question his dedication. And now he needed to show Amalia he would do a strong job speaking up for her art.

This time, he touched her forearm. "Sounds like a deal."

"Great. Then, to go back to your earlier question, I want you to show me your writing when you take me on a date."

His mind flooded with ideas about roses and candlelight and the kind of fancy clothes that no one wore eating out in Honey Wine. Did anyone around rent out limos? Was there a fair coming to town so he could woo her with funnel cake and feats of strength? "A date."

"Yep. That's your assignment. Plan us a date. Or—you know what, pick something you've done in the past for a first date, and set that up for us. Just be sure it's something where I can read your journal, so no movie theaters."

Or limos, he figured. Amalia was too dynamic for a normal small town date, but he had to remember she wasn't saying she wanted to go out with him for real. It was all part of her scheme to discover how he always went wrong. "Got it."

"Okay." She stood, and he followed suit.

For a sec, he was near dizzy with the reminder of how much shorter she was. Like sitting side by side, talking over all these needs and desires of theirs, had evened them up. Their standing reminded him of how she managed to fill such a towering amount of space, despite her actual stature.

Before he could make his thanks and retreat, Amalia touched a finger to his wrist. "Want to seal the deal with a hug?"

He lifted his head and smiled. A hug, he could manage, and never mind all the ways he wanted to get back into his truck and spend the drive home pondering everything. Amalia's palm on his side was so steady. So grounding.

So much a reminder that she wanted him to do well, and that all he wanted, in that moment, was everything Amalia wanted.

⇢⇉⇉♥⇇⇇⇠

It engulfed her, Dante's hug. Not that surprising, what with his height and long arms and broad chest all working together to wrap her in his warmth.

She sank in, noticing stuff like the faint scent of lavender on his shirt, and the ambient rumble-rasp noise of her ear settling against his pecs, and the flex of his palms on her back. Neither of them moved to break apart, to evaluate the moment, to call the deal sealed.

It's possible they'd have remained at her kitchen bar, discovering new ways for their torsos to jigsaw together, if Amalia hadn't glanced past Dante and found her brother and grandmother watching from the doorway.

"Hey there, sis. Not interrupting, are we?" Adrian's voice was the sing-song of insufferable siblings everywhere.

Dante startled, then shifted his palms to her shoulders. It was nearly platonic. Almost not worth teasing her about, if Adrian hadn't already seen them wrapped around each other. Amalia dropped her forehead to his chest, muttering, "Familia."

Adrian rounded the counter, ruffling her hair as he passed. "Me and Aubuela are on our way home from the store, but she wanted to stop and see you. Since it's been a while and all." He helped himself to the rest of the chips and salsa, winking before digging in.

Abuelita accepted Amalia's kiss and grasped her hands. "Mija, if we'd known you were busy with a friend …" Her mild words didn't match the way she was sizing up Dante.

"Friend," muttered Adrian. "Right."

Dante gave her brother a napkin and a pointed look, which did at least prompt Adrian to swipe up the crumbs he'd spewed.

"Is he more than a friend, then? Porque no me dijiste que estas dating." Abuelita's eyes twinkled, because Adrian didn't get his tendency for mischief out of nowhere.

Amalia pressed her lips together, then stood back enough to create a circle of everyone. "We're not dating. Dante Morales, this is my big brother Adrian, and our granny, Elena Hidalgo."

He bent to kiss the cheek Abuelita presented. "Señora, mucho gusto."

"Morales? You related to Leo and Enrique?"

Before answering Adrian, Dante gave her a resigned look. Amalia wasn't as convinced as Dante was that his cousins had spread a bunch of gossip about his bedroom skills, but she could tell he was braced for anything.

Always a good idea, where her brother was concerned.

Dante sighed. "Yeah, they're my primos."

Adrian scooped up a glob of salsa and crunched away, wiggling his eyebrows.

She turned away from the men. "You should text me next time you want a ride to the market." Normally her mom opted to run her granny on her errands, but her parents were on vacation. It surprised her that her brother had been roped in, instead of their aunt, or Amalia herself.

Abuelita waved her off. "He took me out to the Costco, he was going anyway. Plus you are always so busy with your work. Commissions, expos, I can't keep up. Never time for a social life, never time for family errands. I saw that calendar in your hallway. Some day, you will look up and it will be too late to find love."

Was it a comfort that Abuelita used the same lines on her, even after walking in on her and Dante? If nothing else, it made it easier to deploy the response she'd honed to counter the accusation that she was wasting her time. "Some day, you'll all look up and understand that my dedication is how I earn the success my art deserves."

"Art won't keep you warm at night," Abuelita said, but her tone had softened. Amalia could feel the fondness in it—and the recurring familial message that she couldn't be happy without a man in her life. Funny how no one ever harped on her big brother to settle down. In her family, only the unmarried women were incomplete.

And then her granny turned to Dante. "This one looks like a fine bed-warmer, so. We will leave them to it, Adrian. Vamos."

※⇒⋙♥⋘⇐※

At the click of the closing door, Dante returned to the stool. Gave her space to process, or retreat, or whatever she needed.

"So that happened," she said. He missed the color her voice usually held.

"Yep."

"And now you know my granny and my brother."

He grimaced. "Yep."

"Was that okay?"

But he didn't want to sidetrack them talking about Adrian's insinuations. He'd heard them all before, in words more cleverly targeted to stick under his skin. "Nothing to worry about. Are you … is your family going to give you problems?"

She shrugged. "Nothing beyond the usual."

Something slithered through him. Something like a scratch in his throat, except it went all through his chest. He wanted to know what she meant by the usual. Wanted to figure out how she felt about that usual, and if there was anything he could do to turn her usual into something that made her days glow.

"I'm thinking," Dante started. He watched her eyes fix on him, sharp and steady. "What she was talking about, your work—"

"Dante." Amalia's tone was clipped.

Maybe his face flushed again—he was going to let his beard grow up his cheeks so she wasn't constantly seeing his blushes—but she sent a slightly tense nod his way and pushed away from the counter.

"Let's sit in the living room. Leave all that."

He set the bowls and cups in the sink, then followed her. She'd settled into one of her off-beat chairs. He returned to the green one with the fringy pillows, pressing back a small smile at how it felt comfy now. Like all he had to do was sit in a place twice for it to become a little bit his own welcome spot.

"Look, my family is my job to handle. They don't make a difference to our deal. Same way you're the one who has to figure out how to make your cousins stop bad-mouthing you, if you plan to."

"Got it." He didn't like it, but he got it. And her attitude broadcast clear as spring rain that she wasn't open to talking it out. Not yet, anyway. "You never said, what's the proposal for FoundersFest?"

"I did."

"You said inclusion. I don't know what that means, though. As vendors?"

FoundersFest was an annual July weekend of events designed to bring tourists to Honey Wine. Food stalls, games, folk dance demonstrations and a competition, craft booths and food and all kinds. He always got involved with setting up Town Square and the various tents, having been roped in by a couple of guys from the trades unions. The whole thing was about the Czech migration into central Texas, so it was a lot of polka and kolaches and quilts and sausages.

She shook her head, maybe banishing family stuff as much as answering him. "Yeah, no. Not just vendors, but recognizing that Honey Wine wasn't founded solely by the Bohemians. I got the idea a couple of years back. I was in the shade tent watching Ellie teach people to play Taroky—she was talking about the history of tarot card games, and it got me searching up the history of Loteria. Which is older, for the record. So then I'm looking around and thinking about all the stuff from our culture that's been here just as long, or longer, than everything else at FoundersFest."

He almost shrugged, cause it was no surprise to him to find a Eurocentric narrative for the heritage stuff that made people show up for three days of festivities. But then he noted the way her mention of Loteria had sent a smoothing kind of comfort down the back of his head. Like the idea of both games filling the shade tent made his own mind more expansive. It was some kind of magic, and he ended up grinning at Amalia. "That's so true."

"Glad you agree."

"With historical fact? Yeah, revolutionary."

Amalia made one of those scoffing noises, which he took to mean: welcome to our modern reality. But she settled into talking over her proposal, too, and promised to send over her documents for him to take on board as he set about talking to the gatekeepers who hadn't, so far, given her ideas a foot in the door.

Finally she stretched and said, "Okay, I have stuff to do. Text me in the next couple of days about that date."

He wondered, as he re-fluffed the pillows he'd crushed and headed towards her door, if they were on cheek kiss terms. If now they'd gone and gotten physical with that first hug, more physical stuff would follow. But she just stood back and said, "Bye," and he found himself giving her a nod and heading for his truck, without any further contact at all.

CHAPTER 5

Dante called Mike Moll the next day. "I had an opening. You still need me to come by about the sink, or did you find someone else?"

Mike put on his usual bit of bluster, but Dante knew a relieved voice when he heard one. No one alerted him, when he went to his apprenticeship, how quickly he'd learn to recognized when a customer was on the edge of panic. It turned out to be one of those things that came along with learning to read blueprints and install backwater valves.

He ended up at the gallery just before closing. By the time he'd replaced the cracked pipe and tightened all the joints, Mike was drifting around the space. Maybe he needed to do the little tidying tasks, or maybe he was making work for himself while he waited Dante out; either way it just about reeked of fidgety energy. If he liked the guy any better, he'd recommend Sheila's slow flow class.

Maybe he oughtn't to withhold good advice based on interpersonal vibes, but even before he'd seen how Mike treated Amalia, Dante'd found him a bit of a pillbug.

"All done." Dante wiped his hands on a handkerchief. "Sink shouldn't be giving you trouble again."

"Thanks," Mike nodded.

"Here you are," he said, passing over his tablet to let Mike tap in his authorization to pay. Dante was tempted to leave it at that, but more tempted by the idea of having good news to report back to Amalia. "So, didn't your mom used to carry Amalia Reyes's pieces when she ran the place?"

Mike's lips pursed. "A time or two. They didn't fit so well into our usual offerings. Even more so, since I've streamlined according to what's profitable and popular with our customer base."

"Looks like you have all kinds of art." Dante waved his arm at the paintings and ceramics and prints and sculptures filling the space. Maybe he didn't get what streamlining meant, but if Mike wanted to explain it to him, he'd play nice in hopes of smoothing the way for Amalia's goals.

"I carry several mediums that all appeal to the consumer who wants a fine piece to commemorate their visit to Honey Wine and to celebrate the beauty and traditions of the Texas Hill Country." Mike nodded at Dante's toolbox. "You got everything?"

"Yeah, thanks."

"Okay, then. Appreciate you finding time for me after all."

Dante watched Mike make another pass around the room, straightening postcard-sized prints in a rack, flipping off the lights in the back half of the gallery.

"You should think about giving her space. Put her in the Art Walk. Let her prove her point about how her work does—what'd you say? Celebrate the traditions of Honey Wine."

"I'm not saying y'all don't have history here," Mike said without looking at him. "It's just not what people come looking for."

His near about ground his teeth to grit. This fucker. "Because you won't let them see what they're missing. You know, your uncle told me your family moved to Texas just before the Second World War. Mine, though? I got roots in the Hill Country going back to before Texas was a Republic."

"I know what my customers want. I know what sells." Mike held the door open, keys inserted to lock the gallery and, Dante figured, escape this conversation.

"You ought to make room for the idea something could surprise you. It's real nice, discovering new things and knowing you help others do the same. You probably think I'm just a plumber, what do I know of that, but I have my opportunities. And you're doing yourself and this town a disservice by closing up your mind about this."

He walked on out to his work van without waiting for Mike Moll to get in any kind of final word.

※※※ ♥ ※※※

> Dante: I might have made things worse with Mike
>
> Dante: sorry
>
> Dante: I'll talk to Bill. Get gnats in his ear

> Amalia: Gnats?

> Dante: Couldn't remember the right phrase. Is it flies?

> Amalia: No idea. I like gnats, let's stick with them

> Dante: ...

> Amalia: I do not care for gnats, in my ear or in general. I like the phrase

> Dante: gnats up your nose is the worst one

> Amalia: the worst

> Dante: Mike is also the worst

> Amalia: All the gnats should go up his nose

Dante: they should

Dante: but sorry if I made it worse with him. I'll get Bill on board, he can get his sister, and she can be a gnat at her son, maybe. Worth a try.

> Amalia: I wasn't expecting success.

Dante: Oh. Right.

> Amalia: Cause it's Mike, not cause it's you

> Amalia: cause he's the worst

He didn't answer, not even after her explanatory follow-up. Amalia stopped herself from checking in on him after another hour of silence. It wasn't her job to comfort his insecurities. Maybe to help him *confront* the insecurities, but it was on him to process himself through what that meant. She had commissions to finish up. She'd have plenty of time to joke around with him when she wasn't using a stone point to add dimension to the sky portion of her latest creation.

She sank into the work, uninterrupted by text notifications. The music in her earbuds only cut off when her aunt called.

"Cariño, how are you?"

"Tía Cecily, what's going on?" She set the grinder back on her workbench and powered everything down. Calls with her aunt were never brief interruptions. Sure enough, by the time she'd shucked her gloves and goggles, her aunt had was only halfway through the roster of what her kids were up to and what she'd thought about Amalia's parents' vacation texts.

She'd swept up the filings with her shop rag and was jotting a reminder about an adjustment she wanted to make to the foreground tree branches by the time Cecily said, "And Mama says you have a new man?"

Amalia leant against her workbench and crossed her arms. "Yeah, no."

"She described him as, and this is a direct quote, 'muy guapo.'"

Dante's looks were nice enough, even to someone more discerning than her granny, but he still wasn't her boyfriend. She forced herself to unclench and do the upper back stretches that kept her mobile enough for her long hours at the bench. "He's a friend. We barely hugged that once, and since my brother barged in and embarrassed us, I'm sure it'll never happen again."

She was sure it would, but she was also sure she needed the family chatter to fixate on someone else's life. "Tía, tell me, what are you doing yourself these days, now my cousins are scattered to all the winds?"

"Oh, I manage to keep busy. Did I say I'm helping with the retirement party for your tío's boss?"

Amalia could practically see Cecily waving off the question. As always. "But what about something just for you? You said you might start making pottery again?"

"Oh, well," Cecily said, her voice wry, but not particularly sorrowful. "That's a lot of mess and bother. Besides, I'm sure I wouldn't be any good anymore."

Amalia sighed. Tempting her aunt back to her creativity was like trying to pierce 12 gauge steel with a thumbtack. Everyone in the family had one of her gorgeous glazed bowls or vases prominent in their homes, but she'd stopped making decades earlier, after her second kid was born. It always broke Amalia's soul that everyone else, including her aunt, thought it was perfectly fine that caretaking had taken precedence over all other aspects of Cecily's life. "I have this friend, her main work is these kind of fantastical planters, lots of folkloric influence. Anyhow, she's running a weekend hand-building workshop coming up soon. Want me to send you the info?"

"No, thank you, mija. It sounds too involved for me. Maybe you and this young man of yours should do something like that. Or one of those painting and drinking classes. See if he's the kind to appreciate how hard you work on your sculptures."

The grim thing was, Tía Cecily thinking Amalia should be with someone who supported her art was a step forward in their ongoing conversation. For too long, her family talked as if Amalia would follow the path of her aunt. Or her dad's mom who'd been a reporter until she got married. Or her big cousins who stopped acting in local dramas once they had kids. Even the one who'd met her husband at their community theatre; he'd never stopped performing, and she spent his rehearsal time wrangling their four-year-old on her own.

So it was frustratingly novel for anyone to expect Amalia to maintain both her career and her relationship. She'd spent years encouraging her female relatives to maintain space for their individual pursuits, only to hear a thousand iterations of, 'until you have a family of your own, you can't possibly understand the choices I make.' As if being an individual, with her own creative passions and other interests, was less important than the sacrifices of caretaking.

It was a crumb of progress, for her aunt's message to morph to, 'maybe you can make the choices you claim are so important to you, if you find a supportive enough partner.' Cecily wasn't changing her attitude towards the value of her own pursuits, at least not in any kind of actionable way, but each millimeter of concession felt significant.

Even if the concession was only apparent when her family thought she was weakening in her anti-relationship stance. Which could mean they were just waiting for her to fall into some love-altered state where she would abandon her career and her principals and her own interests, in favor of proving that they'd been right all along.

She'd taken a trip with her friend Patti once, carting their portfolios around to galleries in San Antonio and Austin, and mentioned the pleasure of being free of family pressure for a few days. Patti suggested she just move—Amalia was moving from stability to comfortable success with her career just then.

What she'd explained to Patti, and reminded herself of when she got too frustrated, was that she only had to fight her stance so hard because she saw her family all the time. Their brand of pressure lessened with the miles, but so did the joy Amalia got at being near them. It was a calculation she'd made, and the joy far outweighed everything else. And so, in her stubborn way, she fought.

She sent her kisses along to Cecily's family, and walked out to putter in her garden a bit. Gave her irritation a chance to settle, and her eyes a rest, before returning to her workbench with her vision firmly in place.

CHAPTER 6

"What did you pack us?"

Dante's half-tilt smile graced his face, and he slid the cooler towards her. They were perched on the tailgate of his truck, near the banks of the Blanco River.

Dante had planned a picnic lunch date, knocking off work early and picking up Amalia—and her yoga supplies so they could head to class after—and she couldn't fault his romantic impulses. Before them, a field of early spring wildflowers was blooming, all pink and yellow and orange fluttering in the breeze. She knew a swath of bluebonnets would emerge within weeks if not days, covering the opposite bank with brilliant, iconic blooms.

Amalia opened the lid and discovered a neatly packed jigsaw of containers. A selection of cheeses, a stack of assorted crackers, grapes, nuts, brownies. Cool cans of soda in each corner. "Sweet."

"Am I?"

It was no effort to nudge her elbow into his arm. "Yes, Dante, you did good. I plan to compliment you when you deserve it, but you have to believe me when I do. Or is the problem that one of your flaws is not being able to accept the praise you're seeking out?"

He watched a pair of dragonflies take off towards the shade of a gnarled live oak. "Yeah. I don't know. Maybe."

"And now you're grumpy again." She took the sleeping bag that he'd offered up as a picnic blanket and hopped down, making for a stretch of grass close to the burbling water.

Dante followed with the cooler. After they'd settled in, he assembled a few cheese-and-cracker sandwiches on her plate, and cracked open his drink.

She let the silence hold for a while, separating out what was going on with her from what her deal was with Dante. Took the kind of cleansing breath Sheila insisted they carry away from the yoga studio, and lifted her face to the sky. "I might be in a mood, myself. My mom called today, about my granny's birthday dinner."

He hummed a questioning kind of encouragement.

"She said I should bring you." She rolled a plump grape between her fingers before popping it into her mouth. "It's not even happening until next month."

"What did you say?"

"Tried to change the subject. She didn't let up. The whole family is convinced we're an item now, and they're fucking delighted about it."

His tilted head and briefly furrowed brow asked her if she wanted to tell him more about why that made her mad. The infuriating thing was, she did.

"It's nothing wrong about you. About anyone I'm in a relationship with, or in what they think is one. It's just their goddamn expectations, and how impossible it is to get them to see that I won't live down to them."

"How would that work? What do they expect?"

Her smile felt dry as the cracker she let fall to her plate.

"They've got ideas about how I—because I'm a woman—need someone to take care of me. And more to the point, someone who I can take care of. It's the part about the women always taking care of others that gets them going. I've never, not once, told them they're wrong, for the way they give up every single thing that matters to their souls in order to turn their homes into, like, cozy little refuges for their husbands and kids and parents and whoever else happens by to take up all their time."

He was regarding her somberly. Like he very much was listening to her, and wanted her to feel free to vent. "Damn. Okay. That's … a lot."

She sighed and looked out over the water, tucking a stray lock of hair back into her hair clip. "Yeah. I'm not saying I didn't benefit from it, the way the whole lot of them do whatever it takes. My tías used to drive me to art classes. My grandparents never missed a school exhibition. My mom …"

Dante made her two more crackers, overflowing with cheese, then stretched out on his elbow. It helped, that he seemed to be watching the clouds move in, instead of her face.

"Thanks," she said. "My parents are the same. Internalized societal expectations, settling into traps that keep women earning less and being more responsible for daily household stuff. This kind of knee-jerk defensiveness about how, since they love each other so much, they shouldn't need to interrogate their own dynamic. Which is fine, if that's what they want."

"Sure."

"Except if I go and express how I need to make my own life free of all that, Mami takes it as an implied criticism, and my dad does the respect your elders bit, and then they're porcupines to hang out with. So, yeah. It is a lot, sometimes, and one of those times is when everyone is hoping I'll bring a nice young man—that's you—to Abuelita's birthday."

"That sucks, I'm sorry. I wish you weren't under that pressure. Would it help, do you think, if you do invite me?"

Amalia fiddled with the tab on her soda. Click, click, click, until it snapped off and fell into the drink. "I haven't figured that out yet."

He sat up and opened the container of brownies. "I get it's not simple. But if it makes it less of a pain for you, I'm happy to go."

Ha. Preparing him for a family party might be too much nonsense to untangle for herself, much less for him. "We'll see. I'll let you know."

He studied her, looking like studying was his new favorite thing, then nodded. "Got it."

She almost believed he did. It was an interesting kind of relief, talking about this stuff with Dante. Normally she only discussed her family pressures with her relatives, and that meant layers upon layers of emotional weight from all sides.

"Okay, I'm starting to think you know more about talking —about listening—than you claimed. Where's all the awkward pauses you assured me filled every date you've ever been on?" She exaggerated, of course. It was his patient silence as much as anything that gave her the space to unload.

He huffed a bit. "I'm not in danger of taking over anyone's conversation. Never have been. But I'm glad if it helped."

"Well, don't let it go to your head." She sat back, arms wrapped around her knees. "No, sorry, do. If you like. You don't deserve my snark. Let's get back to talking about you. Do you think you being a quieter guy is the same thing as having awkward pauses? How does this compare to your normal dating situation?"

She'd assigned him to create this date for them, since he claimed his first dates fizzled out and left him pretty sure he was too boring. A nice picnic at a pretty spot, his seeing to their comfort, even the unexpected space for her to vent a little about one of the weights on her heart—Amalia liked having things to critique, and he wasn't helping her out any.

Dante brushed an ant from his jeans. "I don't know."

She pulled out her phone. He could try to be fidgety and evasive all he wanted, but she'd compiled a list of exploratory questions.

He side-eyed her phone like the threat it was, and rubbed his neck. "Okay, maybe I do know."

Amalia lowered her phone and raised her eyebrows, waiting for him to quit stalling.

"I told you about being shy."

"Sure."

"I get that can turn into an excuse. I try to not let it. I looked up strategies and advice. Eye contact, active listening, making a point to talk to lots of people—this Art Walk project is pushing me there. All that. But Leo said ..." He reached for another handful of nuts. Sorted them out, and, like a monster, tossed the pecans into the field. "Leo is friends with this woman, Jules, we had a date a couple months back. And maybe Leo was exaggerating, or maybe she's not typical of everyone. Maybe and maybe, all the maybes, except what she tells him is that I don't have any conversation. All I did was drink, and criticize her food choices, and ignore her hints about going somewhere after dinner. Stared off into space. And then I asked if she'd have my kids."

Amalia had never been so close to a spit-take in her life. "You what?"

He shrugged. "I mean, that's what Leo reported."

"And I guess that's not what you thought was happening?"

"I thought I was telling her about the good tacos I'd had there."

"The kids thing, though?"

Dante watched the water a moment, then faced her. "I probably said I was interested in family, in settling down. I do tell people that, if we talk about what we want out of dating. Didn't mean for her to take it as any kind of demand."

She took that in. "Yeah. Okay, makes a bit of sense. I can't say how you communicated it all, but I guess her interpretation wasn't out of nowhere."

Another shrug. The man was constructed entirely of shrugs and warmth and muscles and sad eyes. Slowly, he straightened and reassembled the food containers. "I guess I understand that, now. Don't love how Leo tells that story, or the part about how low she rated our end-of-night kiss."

Her brows went up again. "Ouch." Those taunting cousins were relentless.

"Well. Yeah. So that all snowballed until I got the idea—and the nerve—to ask for your help."

"And here we are."

"And here we are," he repeated, but more glum. Pobrecito.

She dusted her hands on her pants and made her voice businesslike. "Okay, great. Now let's see what you're working with."

He swallowed hard. "Sorry?"

"I want a baseline. I don't take Leo's word on anything, so let's do it. Let's kiss. Let me rate your skills for myself."

He lifted his chin a fraction, which seemed mild enough, until she paired it with the way his focus had sharpened on her, eyes alight like a kid in the candy store. The way his fingers curled to his palms, like he feared that if they slackened, he'd reach for everything he'd ever wanted.

Looked like Dante was keen as hell to learn.

She angled towards him and his body jerked, as if he was up for fighting against any restraints she imposed. But also, which was where something entirely wicked and wanting in Amalia took note, as if he was he more than ready for Amalia to attach those restraints in the first place. She moved an inch closer, and the breath gusted out of him like she'd just hauled him the final few feet up a rocky cliff. Some sort of predator within Amalia took notice, and prowled forward. The air sharpened between them, like hot steel.

Amalia took Dante's hand and wrapped it to her waist. A nod was all it took for him to mirror the action on her other hip. His hold was firm, one large hand warm, the other cool from his soda.

Had she noticed his mouth before? The way his neatly trimmed beard framed it? How that crooked incisor set off the way his smile hitched up on one side? The plush cushion of his lower lip? It was all worth noticing. Worth spending several intent seconds studying.

But what Amalia needed to know was: was he worth tasting?

Dante's tongue slipped out and moistened the inner rim of his lips, marking an irresistible landing pad for her mouth. So Amalia did not resist.

That first touch sizzled, everything locking into place. Dante's hands flexing low on her hips, his pleased, eager hum, his firm and welcoming mouth. The feathery slip of his hair through her fingers when she perfected the angle of his head.

It wasn't until she brushed her tongue to his that things began to go south.

It wasn't immediately bad. His breath held the sweetness of chocolate, as probably did hers. His lips continued to be deliciously firm. But then his tongue started darting in and out of her mouth. Not rapidly, but also, not sensually.

If there existed a sensual way to kiss while imitating a Komodo dragon scenting the air with its forked tongue, Amalia was not aware of it.

She pulled back, and was glad to see Dante's tongue retreat as he opened his eyes.

"Hey, there." He sounded almost proud of himself.

She pressed her lips together. It didn't do much to rid her mouth of the feel of him. "Dante."

The smile faded from his expression as gradually as it so often appeared. He dropped his hands from her waist and made to stand up, but she pressed his shoulders to keep him with her. "Hey, no running off."

"I wasn't going to strand you here."

"I know you weren't. But you were going to, like, mentally or emotionally flee the scene. And you shouldn't. It wasn't that bad."

CHAPTER 7

Wasn't. That. Bad.

Okay.

Okay, okay. It wasn't a new verdict on him. Not one he'd heard directly from the source, and could be he'd harbored some hopes that the reports weren't so correct.

Now he knew they were. So. Good news.

Amalia said his name again, and he decided it was not in a pitying tone. She was sometimes abrupt, but she wasn't rude.

He crossed his legs—because he wasn't going to cross his arms—and settled in to pay attention. "Yeah, sorry. Tell me."

"So ... actually, let's back up some. Did you write out those stories like I suggested? Did your Jules experience make it onto the page?"

He blamed the breeze for the little shudder than ran through him. "Yeah. Yes, I wrote things down, yes, some of it was about that date. Mostly recounting our conversation, and what I was trying to say, and what Leo says I said."

"Did you bring your journal?"

He still didn't cross his arms. "No. I decided not to. After I wrote it out, it seemed like showing you would be telling secrets out of bed. Didn't feel right."

Amalia pursed her lips, thoughtful. "All right, I can see

that. And I totally don't want to invade anyone's privacy. The reason I suggested writing it out was from a brainstorming system—getting all the info on the page before trying to organize it. Not creating a narrative until you have the ideas in front of you, then seeing how it fits together."

"Sure."

"So, I guess, if you read it over, did anything new come up? Did you see a pattern?"

He kept his palms on his knees. "I thought I saw a pattern that I don't converse well, but now you tell me I'm okay there. And I thought maybe I'm, I don't know, an uninspired kisser. And now you're going to tell me it's worse than that."

"Dante." If that wasn't what Amalia sounded like when she pitied someone, he was going to have to spend more time figuring her out.

"It's fine. That's why we're here."

"Look." She inched closer, speaking more briskly, and he breathed easier. "Everything was great, to start. But then your tongue got involved, and I know everyone has their own vibe, but your way, Dante, really did not work for me. Think about it. Were you, ya know, with me? Or off on some script in your head?"

Goddamn blushes. She was too clever at seeing into his head. "Maybe the second one."

"Yeah. So. This time, don't jump ahead to what you think comes next. Follow my lead, think about how what I do makes you feel. Think about how I react to what you do. Am I leaning in or tensing up? Mirroring your motions? Be present, just with the two of us, none of the outside noise."

"Got it."

"And for all that's holy, remember that your tongue is not a jackhammer."

Shoulders shaking with laughter, head dropping in embarrassment, he finally wrapped himself up in his arms.

Amalia very much ignored how she'd turned her own damn self on while talking Dante through her kissing philosophy. It wasn't relevant if she was into the idea of some idealized version of Dante getting things right.

The point was to teach him, and then off he would go into that dream future of his. He wanted to improve so whoever was in that future wouldn't need to be the one to fix him. And if she ever wanted a relationship, it wouldn't be with someone she'd needed to train. That smacked too much of the caretaking model she actively avoided.

Not that she wanted a relationship, which is why she'd said no to Dante's asking her last year. His whole vibe was commitment, and that wasn't anything she wanted to get mixed up in.

So: teaching only. And if she managed a buzz from the contact, that was fine. Same as any other casual dating interaction.

"Ready to try again?"

His grin faded again, but this time it was replaced by an intent determination. "Yep. Be in the moment, follow your lead. No jackhammers."

"Exactly." She edged into his space, kneeling between his splayed knees. Like an attentive student, he leaned in when she did. Licked his lips after she did. She could already feel his soft-coarse beard under her palm, even though they'd not yet touched.

And then, they did.

It was better. Much, much better.

Not just because he was echoing her moves, following her hand on his back with his own sliding down her spine. His chest notching closer when her shoulder brushed his pec.

It was something more. Something to do with electrons, maybe.

She slipped her hands around his neck and guided him closer. Their lips mapped each other's contours. He explored her cheek, the slope of her jaw, her mouth again. And when her teeth caught lightly on his sweet lower lip, he opened to her.

Her tongue drifted almost lazily against his, but there was nothing laid-back about pressure of their kiss. Slowly—intentionally; she could feel his intent but also that he wasn't caught up in planning ahead—his returned the favor.

She may have growled a bit. He might have moaned.

Catching herself before she straddled his lap, Amalia led him to slow down, to disengage. To press his forehead to hers, breaths slowing, gazes meeting and moving away in a shy dance.

"Well," she said, and surely he could hear the husky note in her voice.

His breath caught for a second, but he didn't repeat the mistake of gloating before she passed judgment.

She didn't leave him waiting. "Lesson learned. Gold star."

"Whew." His half-grin turned a little sly. "You're a good teacher."

Amalia moved back, and not just so she could retrieve her phone. She didn't need more proof they'd solved Dante's kissing problem. Time to move on to the next issue. She cleared her throat. "Thanks. Glad it worked for you. Tell me this: what are the reasons you want to be in a relationship?"

※※※♥※※※

He coughed. Moved to sit with his knees bent in front of him, cause that kiss—that gold star compliment—the way her pupils were big and captivating. He needed to conceal his crotch. "Sorry?"

"Reasons." She referred to her phone again, all business. "I'm trying to be sure we go at this in an organized way. A way that helps you most. The picnic, the kissing, they're useful exercises, from a mechanical perspective. But if we can dig into your reasons behind it all, I think we can make a smarter plan. So, getting better at sex is one thing, but can you explain why you're so determined about being in a relationship?"

Mechanical.

So much for feeling like, intense as their conversation might get, their rapport was kinda special. At least he could stop worrying about if his dick would interrupt the conversation.

While Amalia twisted her hair to clip it into a bun and turned to sit cross-legged facing him, he put himself into a classroom mindset. Talked it out. "Well, I want to get married. Have a family. My cousins aside, I'm pretty dedicated to my own family; always hoped I'd get to make a life like my parents did. They're always there for each other, you know? Or maybe you don't—I know yours have a different dynamic. Sorry. But, yeah, that's a lot of it. And now I've got a house, a good income, loyal customers. An apprentice I don't need to throw back to the union for being a fool. Also, like you said the other day, I want to go into a relationship knowing … knowing I'll be good for her."

"You're doing pretty good with this communication thing."

He scrunched his face. "Ha."

"No, for real. Maybe all the reflection is paying off, or maybe it's easier on you if you already know the person. Or since you know this isn't a real date, maybe the pressure is off."

Not a real date.

"Yeah. Could be. But, so, those are my reasons."

She nodded. But said, "No. That's not enough."

A tickle of wildflower scent whipped past him on a gust of wind. Those clouds overhead had massed and turned purple and begun to loom. It was all his tension, made real in the sky. "Why? What's wrong with it? I know it takes me too long to learn, but, Amalia, I do. Learn. I learned my way through school, through the ranks at work. Pre-apprentice, apprentice years one two three four five, journeyman, foreman. Specialist. I'm good at learning. And I can be so good at this. Good enough. What's wrong with wanting it?"

For a fleeting moment, she touched his shoulder. "You are good. I'm not arguing you're not. I'm saying, you're talking about the end goal: you, pleasing a wife, in a relationship. I'm asking, though—what's behind that? What makes you want all of those goals?"

"Huh." He wasn't asking her to clarify. Wasn't handing over an instant answer. Was taking the space she'd given him to put together some thoughts.

Of course, it was Amalia, so holding space didn't take top place over her returning to her list of thoughts. She whisked some bug off her pants and kept talking. "So, one thing you took time to mention is, you're stable and housed. Is that important because the security is what matters to you? Or are you looking for, like, the comfort of going home to someone at the end of the day? The connection of sharing space together. Or, is it that you want to be desired in return by someone? That being desirable and appreciated will fill some yearning ache in your soul?"

He probably flinched in some way she clocked. For sure his heart had gone racing at her words.

"Dante, it's not bad to want to be wanted. To value being, I don't know, lusted after, and the person your person wants to text in the middle of the day, and applauded for the nice picnics you pack. I'm asking all this because, if you want a relationship cause you want the shared pleasure of being in the moment with someone, that's one thing to think about. And if you want it for validation, for connection, that's also worth naming. Even if what you're after is checking off the next part of the adulting to-do list, it's fine, so long as you value the relationship itself, whenever it comes along. As long as you're not wanting to use another human as some sort of trophy that shows off your own worthiness."

He would've said something, then, if his throat hadn't turned into a rasp file. She kept naming things in this way that bored holes straight through to his most secretive longings.

And things that shone floodlights on his worst worries. Like how Elizabeth's parting shot, when moving out, was about his using her to prove something to himself.

Amalia took his single nod as proof he'd heard her. "Take time on it," she said. "It's not anything you need to know instantly. Honestly, thinking about all this, about how to help you, I realized I could—I should—put some of the same questions to myself. Not that I'm looking for the same things as you, marriage and all, but it's good, right? To understand the underlying parts about what motivates us?"

Dante fought his way past the damning, echoing words about showing off his own worthiness, to say, "You're right. You're smart as hell, which isn't a shock, but. When I get over being poleaxed by your question, I'll let you know."

She flopped back to stare at the sky. "Only if you want to. If it turns out to be something you need to keep private, that's fair."

He let himself flop alongside her. Let himself feel the gentle warmth radiating off her, and that breeze that kept playing at them. And the first drops of a spring rain, unfurling from the clouds like they didn't mind giving him and Amalia just enough warning to pack up and get to the truck before filling the field with water.

CHAPTER 8

> Amalia: Do you read much?

> Dante: Some, yeah. I like detective novels.

> Amalia: Like thrillers?

> Dante: Like Lord Peter Wimsey and Maisie Dobbs.

> Amalia: huh

> Amalia: okay, I looked them up - if you like cosy stuff set before WWII try Phryne Fisher

> Dante: I did, but for Phryne I like the show better

> Dante: what do you read?

> Amalia: never mind, hang on, I'm calling

She let him assure her he had space to talk before starting in. "I read mostly space operas and sci-fi romance, but that's not why I called. There's this great book about sexuality—it's mostly about cis women, but point is, there's info in there about different aspects of sex and sensuality and how the biology and brain stuff interact. I think you should read it. Or listen, if you're an audiobook person. Dr. Emily Nagoski, *Come As You Are*. You'll check it out?"

"I ... yeah." He sounded distracted. "Hang on."

"You said you were free to chat." Maybe she sounded sharp, but here she'd been doing all this thinking about his issues, and coming up with creative solutions, and kissing the man. Was it too much to expect him to pay attention?

She heard the thunk of a car door closing. "I am. I just wanted to get somewhere quieter."

"The audio is in case you're more of an aural learner. Since you did a nice job listening to me about the kissing."

His huff of a laugh was a funny sound, over the phone connection. "I'm glad you thought so. What's the title again?"

She told him, spelled out the author's surname. "There are quizzes and checklists in there, but skip around where you like. My idea is that it'd be handy for us to have some terms in common. Plus, well."

Dante waited a sec before asking, "Well, what?"

Amalia grinned, wondering if he would blush when she kept talking. If he would hide in his vehicle for a bit, cooling down, before getting back to whatever work he'd been doing when she called. "You told me about watching porn to learn sex skills, but that didn't work for you."

He laughed for real. "It's given me a lot of ideas over the years. But not ones I've been able to use for ... education. Not the kind of education that leads to me having happy partners."

"Once again, we can point the blame at society's overwhelmingly male gaze. Which isn't to say there's not more instructive stuff out there. They say if you can think of it, porn has filmed it."

"Believe me, I've looked," Dante muttered. She wondered how much he wanted to get off this call. Too bad; the honesty and refusal to be prudish were good practice for him.

"Anyway, my thinking is that us finding you different porn isn't likely to be a solution. If you learned by watching, I'd never have been subjected to that tongue thing you did."

His groan cracked her up. "I said I'm sorry."

"It's in the past. Plus, it let us see that you can learn with my excellent guidance, and practice. So that's why I thought of the book. After you get ahold of it and go through a few chapters, let's meet up again and figure out what's next."

⇢⋙♥⋘⇠

He finished his last job faster than expected, and was cleaned up and ready to talk to Amalia a bit earlier than she'd said he should come over.

Ready to kiss her, too, if she'd be at all curious how he was doing remembering her lessons. It'd been over a week since the picnic, but he'd been real dedicated to remembering exactly how she softened and arched and hummed in his arms.

He found her still in her workshop, which he'd not properly explored before. She'd bought a couple of acres from a development group that was turning a farm into housing lots. Her property held the barn, which she'd converted into a studio with a dedicated showroom, and put her own house off to the side. Driving into her lot, past her sculptures lining the frontage, the barn was the obvious center of things.

It had a well-sloped roof, too. He could turn it into the catchment area for her rainwater system, if there was room behind it for the tank.

Amalia was running her angle grinder, so he planted himself in the doorway to admire the work underway. Caught himself admiring her a bit, too, but that was natural enough. Even people he'd never kissed, he noticed the sinuous, strong way they moved. The way they occupied their space like it was easy to be in their bodies. Their pert asses in work wear.

Or, could be, he noticed that stuff only about Amalia. All this homework of hers, he kinda got pictures of her in his head when contemplating the bits and pieces of it all.

She set aside the tool and stepped back, looking at her work. It was one of her sheet metal sculptures, six or seven feet high and maybe three wide. Most of the top two-thirds was a tree, which clung to the edge of a cliff. Some roots trailed down along the cliff edge, wrapping around boulders and rocks. Some birds disappeared off into a corner of the sky. It felt very present, very real, for all that the shapes were blockier and the details sparser than in nature.

"That's nice."

Amalia turned, gave him a once-over, nodded. "Thanks."

As he moved closer, he spied more elements. A hint of water below the cliff, some kind of critter occupying the lower branch of the tree. "That a cougar?"

"Nope. It's Mittens."

He laughed. Mittens was the Maine Coon cat their friends Livia and Greg had domesticated. "Serious?"

She set her protective gear on a shelf and wiped down the piece. "Nah, it is a jaguar. I just borrowed Mittens's attitude to the world when shaping it."

When she used her polishing cloth to blot her forehead, Dante closed the distance between them. "Here."

She took the clean handkerchief he'd fished from his back pocket. "I'll muck it up."

"That's the point of a hankie."

Amalia's expression went somewhere soft. Not for long, but it blazed into a permanent image in his mind. Dante didn't mind it.

She didn't even object when he took it back and rubbed clear a smudge on her neck. Or when she tried to tuck it in her coverall, but he guided her hand to stick it back in his own jeans.

"Accelerator."

He flat-out beamed. "Yeah?"

Amalia rolled her eyes a bit, but nodded. "Yeah."

"Been doing my homework." He'd listened to a lot of the book while driving between job sites. Now whenever he arrived somewhere, he pulled out his notebook and wrote down a few thoughts before moving on to looking at his client notes.

So when Amalia said, 'accelerator,' Dante understood. She was telling him that his handing over the clean cloth was something that revved the sensual engines of her brain.

Some people would be turned on—not in a rampant kind of way, just in a *this seems fun* way—by other things. Dancing. Scents. Wearing things that make them feel comfortable or confident. Compliments from someone they trusted.

Dante's own list, so far, was half-formed ideas he caught floating around his mind while he was knee-deep in a job—soft fabrics, solid muscles, in jokes—but they didn't coalesce into a list once he was back in his truck. He'd tried again back at home. No customers nearby, no work interfering with his thoughts. Even then, he didn't come up with the words.

Probably it meant something, how he could make notes about other people, and about ideas he was learning in the book, but not about himself.

Probably he had to tell Amalia about it.

He contented himself with understanding something more about her, and with the glow of having stumbled upon it just by following his impulses. Barely a couple of weeks into this deal of theirs, and he could ID his positive changes.

"Okay, star student, you showed up too early. I'm going to clean up for real; you can let yourself into my place and I'll find you when I find you."

Dante ended up sprawled across Amalia's couch, flipping

through pages of his notes. He'd brought the spiral in with him, grabbed a beer from her fridge to keep him occupied while she closed down her shop for the day.

He tried Amalia's method of looking for patterns, and right off noticed he'd written a lot about the idea of accelerators. And not much about the brakes, which were whatever moments or thoughts that took people out of the sexy space.

It wasn't the existence of brakes that threw him—he'd figured out that he was either all gas, or all brakes, so A-plus to the book for teaching him something. But he was stuck over the advice about learning to ease off the brakes when he encountered them, instead of coming to a dead stop.

Maybe he needed a clutch. Some way to get himself in neutral. So far, nothing he'd read taught him how to do that.

On one end of things, he was supposed to accept that there was nothing wrong with him. That his way of approaching sex was normal. Acceptable.

So he'd written, "It's okay for me to be how I am."

And put a big star off in the margin to be sure he could find those words again when he needed them. Cause it was nice to know, even if he had to work at it, that he wasn't, in himself, a problem.

Even if he also had to learn, not just his own engine, but that other people were real different—from each other, and from him. And it didn't seem like others would enjoy being with him, if they ever tried to put on their brakes when he was so gassed up he didn't catch their signals.

He set the notebook aside and took a long pull on his bottle, looking around Amalia's space. The late afternoon sun streamed in her windows, doing that nice dance of light across her concrete floor. A big rug filled the sitting area, with a couple of fluffier ones anchored between the seats and coffee table. The other end of the sofa was piled with pillows and blankets, and that side of the table held a stack of books and some sort of yarn project. On Dante's side, all was clear.

He'd had to rescue a coaster from between two novels to set down his beer.

It almost was like she'd created an empty space for him to fill.

Or like she was used to making her nest where she liked it, how she liked it. And like he was the wrong one for chasing a sense of balance every time he repositioned his two matching cushions on either side of his own sofa.

He flipped through the notebook again, stopping at the start of a list. Clicked open his pen and wrote down more.

Ideas and things that turn me on:

- bare, strong arms
- making her laugh for real
- when she asks me out
- that fancy dark eyeliner thing like her eyes are wings
- confidence (it's also scary? Figure this out)
- getting my shirt ready for a date
- she texts me when I didn't expect it
- boobs, obviously
- Amalia's brain

In his defense, before he was sitting in her space, waiting for her, adding to the list she prompted him to make, he hadn't noticed how the most specific turn-ons he could name were extremely specific to Amalia.

⁂

"What's that?"

Dante jerked, and slammed his notebook shut.

She bit back a smile, knowing he'd likely heard her amused snort.

"Hush," he grumbled. "It's unfair to laugh when you know I'm embarrassed."

"Are you?" She perched on the arm of the sofa. He'd written his name and 'World History' in thick ink on the cover, but it looked fairly unused. There were ragged edges from where pages were ripped from the spiral, but only a few. "You've had that since high school?"

"Should I have thrown out a perfectly good notebook?"

"No, but I'm guessing your history teacher wanted you to use it back then."

He flushed even more. "I switched to another one for class."

Amalia reached over and thumbed the pages—not enough to read his words, but enough to see that it looked like a perfectly average school supply. "Why?"

Seeming reluctant, Dante unfisted the hand pressing the cover closed. He lifted then resettled his shoulders. "Someone said red notebooks are for math, and history should be yellow. I didn't know that before, but when I looked around class, that's what everyone else had. Or lots of people did, I guess. My math notebook was purple that year, but some others also had purple, so I didn't change to red until the next year."

He didn't explain whatever else the switch to a yellow notebook had entailed. If he had allowance to pay for it; if he needed a ride to the store; if he copied over the words from the red spiral to the yellow one, or taped the torn-out notes into the fresh spiral.

Somehow, she knew he'd accomplished the change as quietly as possible. A swift slide away from the discomfort of not fitting in, without stopping first to question who it was dictating the correct colors of subject notebooks, or why it mattered that he follow those arbitrary rules.

Dante, she was beginning to see, kept himself in the background until he felt assured that he would fit in.

She stood. "Another beer?"

He shook his head. "Not yet. I can order that pizza now, if you're ready."

She left him to it and went to change out of her work clothes. After a quick shower, she threw her hair into a braid and detoured through her kitchen for a drink of her own.

Amalia returned to find Dante still on the couch, red notebook open on his lap.

"Hey." She settled in beside him, close enough to read if he was willing to tilt his words her way. "So, you ready to talk about it?"

"Ugh."

She nudged him with her knee. "I didn't tell you to come over cause I won't eat a whole pizza on my own. You're the one with the goal here."

"You have a goal, with the art show."

She nudged him again. "A goal that requires some face time with me, then."

Dante nodded, real slow, but shifted the spiral so it rested across both their laps. "Okay. Yeah. So."

She waited for more.

And waited.

Before she shoved away and told him off—he was the one supposedly so eager to learn that he'd interrupted the end of her work day—he pushed air between his lips and asked, "Can we try kissing again?"

CHAPTER 9

This whole thing of recognizing his brakes and trying to stop riding them chafed. He didn't like connecting the grumbling in his gut with the way he'd had to muster up nerve to ask for a kiss.

According to his homework, it was okay. His engines could rev wildly when someone approached him—and what was so wrong about knowing he was desired? Nothing, that's what. It didn't have to be a big deal that what Amalia called his 'duckling to swan' journey had left him with some insecurities about his appearance. So that was fine.

Also, it was fine if voicing his desires applied his brakes. If speaking up shut him down. That was normal, too. A good idea for him to know about it, to work on how to circumvent the problem, but: normal.

And he didn't need Amalia attuned to the way his desire operated. She wasn't interested in a relationship with some tied-to-his-hometown guy. Maybe she was working to expand her recognition in Honey Wine for now, but with her big talent, her big ambition, she'd outpace the place soon enough. And meanwhile, all he'd be would be more settled down.

"Or, we can skip it. Talk about the book, like you said." Except he'd been doing so much thinking about the kiss.

About if he'd really improved as much as she'd said. If his new skills had stuck. And if she had more notes for him.

If she'd felt any of the same shivers that had gone down his own spine.

"No," she said, shifting a tiny mite closer. "We can kiss. I put on the deadbolt, so there's no chance my brother will walk in on us."

He chuffed out a laugh that, maybe, hid how his mouth had gone dry. "Good. Smart. Thanks."

He sipped his beer. She sipped hers.

"Should I start?" He wiped his palms on his thighs. Wriggled his toes to expel some of his tension. Studied every curve of her neck and her jaw and her lips.

Her lips, which twitched up at the corners. Her eyes, crinkled like she found his hesitation somewhat appealing. And then she was leaning into him, her lips opening his. His hand fisted her braid, lightly, like it was a lifeline there in case he needed it as he dove into the experience of intimacy with her.

Amalia pulled him closer, taking charge of their pace and intensity, and Dante sank under her control. He met her warmth for warmth, pressure for pressure. Mirroring, but also building on her cues.

His pulse raced, but he didn't let the thrumming of his body take over. None of his rapid-fire nonsense now: she'd shown him a rhythm she enjoyed, and he'd done his damndest to memorize it. When he skimmed his palm down to her hip, and she hummed against him, a jolt of satisfaction rushed through him.

He'd done that for her. He'd coaxed out her pleasure, caused her fingers to tighten in his hair, inspired her to press her chest to his.

With a gasp, Dante pulled away. He dropped his head back against the sofa, eyes closed. His chest was heaving, but he couldn't do much about it, not yet.

Nothing but remind himself that Amalia only kissed him

because he'd asked. Because he needed to learn. Needed to never again witness Leo and Enrique in a giggle-fit about rumors that he was crap in bed.

He felt the sofa shift as she moved away. Felt her scoop up his notebook from where it'd fallen between them. Rubbed idly at the spot where the spiral binding had been crushed against his leg.

He'd been so caught up in their kiss, he'd almost forgotten about the notebook. Almost forgotten why they were kissing to start with. Then he'd caught himself exploring the strong curves of her torso, fantasizing about slipping a thumb under her hem to reach her bare flesh, and slammed himself into the remembrance that she wasn't his to explore. She'd approved kissing as a lesson, nothing more. No matter how handsy he felt.

Amalia thumbed the edge of the notebook pages, like maybe she wasn't feeling any kind of anything after that kiss. Her breath didn't saw like his did. She didn't look on the outside like the mess he felt on the inside. "Gonna show me?"

"Sure," Dante said, trying to keep the disappointment out of his voice. Trying not to sound too raw. He flipped past the pages where he'd written about his dating attempts. "Here."

"You write like a draftsman."

"Yep. Trained myself like that when I started my apprenticeship. Easier to work with blueprints and invoices and such if everyone can read each other's handwriting."

She nodded, and he glanced down at the notes he'd taken. The ones she read, following each line of his with her forefinger, pausing to stare across the room like she had to think hard about where he'd written, "I don't need to feel any bad way about the differences between me and anyone else—people are a spectrum. It's normal for me to come when I penetrate someone, but also normal for her not to come that way."

Fucking hell. He should have left the notebook in his truck.

"Hey, listen, it's fine." Amalia tossed the spiral on the coffee table and took up her beer. "The point is for you to learn this kind of thing about yourself. And about sex in general, but for you, specifically, to understand how you operate. It's not like there's a script for being good that doesn't take into consideration your own desires, and those of your partner. Partners. Because there's probably someone out there—or lots of people, I don't know—who would groove just great with the way you're doing things. So what you wrote about being normal? That's important to know. Important for everyone to know. You've done good work."

He nodded. Finished his beer. Resisted checking his phone to track their pizza.

Amalia knocked her knee against his. "So, on top of knowing you're normal, do you get that what works with one partner isn't necessarily going to work with the next? Or even the same woman, but at different times. Hey, I didn't ask—do you only date women? I can't remember otherwise, but could be I'm wrong."

"Yeah, but thanks for checking."

"Sure. Anyway, that's ... okay, for example, with me? I usually like when guys play with my breasts, get all grope-y, you know?"

Double fucking hell. He managed to say, "Sure."

"But then a couple days before my period starts, they're too sensitive for that. So then some guy who thinks he knows my vibe goes and pinches my nipples and I get pissy at him. Cause he's not paying attention to my body language—or my words, but those guys don't get a second chance to start with, so never mind them."

He was minding every one of these guys, but that wasn't his prerogative.

"And that's what I'm saying about context mattering, along with the people involved, with whatever skills or fun they bring to the table. Or the bed."

Looked like the pizza delivery was a few minutes out.

He pulled together another few nerves and said, "Or the sofa."

She snorted. "Sure thing, hot stuff. You did good. We can officially cross kissing off the lesson plan."

He bit his lip a moment. Stopped himself from protesting her approving words. Her praise was a good thing. Kissing was a skill he'd set out to master, and now, hey. He'd done it, to Amalia's satisfaction. To some level way past satisfaction, on his part.

It wasn't her responsibility to keep on kissing him, just cause he liked it so much. Liked pleasing her so much. She hadn't agreed to any more practical demonstrations.

"Cool." He hoisted himself up. "Can I grab another beer? Want one?"

At her nods, he rounded the sofa, dropping a hand to her shoulder in passing. Not sure why. Not sure what he meant by it. Not sure what she thought.

But they settled in with fresh beers, and got working on the pizza, and soon enough it was entirely relaxed and friendly between them. He told her about the videos their friend Greg—owner of the incorrigible Mittens—was helping him compile for a plumbing advice YouTube channel. "He keeps telling me about affiliate marketing and integrations. I'm not trying to monetize like he used to, but he's sure it'll be worth my time. So he's got Johnny—my apprentice, you know—eating up all this filming advice, since he's who's mostly taking the raw footage. I hear too much about raw footage these days. Aspect ratios and such."

"And this is going to make you internet famous?"

"Ha. No. But I've set up a feed—I learned about feeds, and

widgets—to add the videos to my site, and maybe it'll get me more customers like Greg thinks."

"Well, good luck."

"Yeah. If he's right, maybe you'll let me make a video of me installing your rainwater system?"

"Since when am I letting you put that in?"

He gestured to her darkening windows. "You want to establish those fruit trees, you should really have good irrigation in place. Plus, you get the Morales Plumbing pals discount."

"Oh yeah?" She tilted the pizza box towards him, and he waved her off. She slid the last slice onto her plate. "How much of a discount?"

"You cover parts and whatever I have to pay Johnny. For plumbing, not for making content."

She narrowed her eyes, but he still saw the glint in them. "You're really going to need those videos to supplement your income, if you give that kind of deal out to anyone who offers you a couple of beers."

"Yeah, but I'll claim some of your garden harvest, so it balances out in the end."

She scoffed, but also bragged about her current crop of yams and greens.

He found himself saying, "Remember the thing about how other people plant our sexuality gardens, and tend them with their own influences until we're grown enough to take over?"

"From the book? Lots of analogies in there."

"Yeah. This one … it's about how we receive all kinds of messages from growing up—that context you like so much—messages about what's sexy, and what's scary, and what's icky, what we should desire. From family, and community, and, like, school and movies and porn."

She finished off her slice. Waited for him to go on.

"So the idea is, now I'm grown, I've taken over as my own

gardener. I get to redo the landscape to suit myself. Root out invasive shit. Hang a hammock."

She laughed. He accepted, but didn't dwell on, how making her laugh was like routing a perfect flowing stream of clear water. "I don't recall the hammock part of the book. Suppose it's in the index?"

"Might not be."

"Shocking."

He could laugh, too. Even mortified by his ignorance, his living three decades without understanding so much of what shaped him, his constant reminders to himself that wanting to change meant being honest with himself and with Amalia, he could laugh a little, too.

"So what things are your weeds?"

"That I'm trying to root out? I doubt I've found it all yet, but, okay. One thing is feeling like I was unattractive in school, and everyone always talking about who was hot, who was desirable, and knowing that was never going to be me. I think that insecure kid can take over when I'm with someone, and he's so astounded to be making out at all. He's like, 'quick, stick your dick in, before she changes her mind,' which is—whew—not a fun thing to say aloud."

"Damn. I'd guess not. Nice work, though, spotting that."

"Thanks, it's ..." He trailed off. "It's an interesting thing to know. And mixed up in all that is the way we talked about hot girls in school, and the way no one got called out on it, how objectifying them was, for real, dismissed as locker room talk. And then that *Access Hollywood* tape and I'm asking my mamá make me my own pink pussy hat to go march against Trump with her, and of course I'm mad when she tells me stuff about her own experience, but I'm also barely an adult, you know?"

Amalia's toe prodded the yarn project on her coffee table. "That's when I learned to knit. My Tía Cecily tried to teach me when I was younger; she thought it would be a practical kind of thing to do with my artistic side. So I got mad and refused, because it was more of the same old thing about trying to fit me into a domestic sphere. Or that's how I saw it, until I wanted to use my talents for something that felt bigger."

He sat forward and pressed his palms into his eye sockets. "Fuck, it's everywhere, isn't it?"

"What is?" Amalia touched his shoulder, which was damn kind of her, and he sank back to face her.

"You and me, we were both protesting, right? For lots of reasons, but it started with that disrespect, that blatant misogyny. With having to look at phrases like 'locker room talk' and see them for the toxic shit they are. And I listened to the women I love, I believe their stories, and I decide to just not be that kind of asshole if I can help it. Put on my pink hat. So damn proud of being a good man, and it's not until now that I realize: I left it to that woman I love most to knit for me. Didn't think twice about expecting her to give her time and skill to work for me. Didn't even cross my mind to make my own hat. I thanked her, sure, but I didn't see how I was reinforcing gender roles she probably never asked for. And that, right there—that's the invasive shit that's everywhere in this garden of mine."

"It's like bamboo. Impossible to kill."

"Encouraging." He was drawing little circles on his sternum. Maybe he had heartburn, but most likely it was emotions, not his pizza consumption, that had his body acting out of control. "I don't care for knowing I'm such a stereotype."

Amalia crossed her arms like she was getting down to business. "We're describing ourselves as normal, Dante, not stereotypical."

"Same difference."

She was shaking her head before he finished speaking. "Context, again. To me, anyway, normal doesn't sound like a judgement. Stereotypical does. But it's how you interpret it that matters."

"Yeah." He nodded a little. "Okay. I'll think about that."

"Good. Now, fess up: what kind of porn do you like?"

And like that, they were both collapsed back on the sofa, laughing together, and his whole self felt more settled than he'd been since asking for Amalia's help in the first place.

CHAPTER 10

He wasn't quick, and he didn't always see what was coming his way, but Dante was big enough to fill the net, and deft enough to accurately throw back any balls he managed to stop. So when Lee was on the road, Dante was his rec league team's substitute goalie.

He was late; he'd overslept. It wasn't the beers he and Amalia'd shared. No, it was a gross kind of mental hangover, from thinking too much about his damn metaphorical garden.

Their game was at an exurban park north of town, off the Austin road. It had well-maintained fields, and terrible parking. He was about ready to give up and head to the strip mall a ten minute jog away, when he caught sight of his cousins' bikes. He popped out of his truck, wrestled them to the top of the space they filled, and squeezed his truck in behind them. If he had to oppose Leo and Enrique's team, the least they could do was make room for him. Not that he was making a point to tell them they'd done so. Not when they'd gone and rushed him as soon as Leo noticed him putting on his gloves.

"Dante." Enrique wrapped him in one of his energetic hugs, trying as always to lift him into the air. Failing, as always, but grinning about it.

Leo reached up and tried to mess with his hair.

Dante shoulder-checked him then planted a kiss on his forehead. "Y'all ready to lose?"

"With you in goal? As if." Leo said, his crinkled eyes suggesting he was settling in for a round of nonsense. "I've heard all about how you can't read a signal."

"I don't know, bro, he's pretty good at stopping people from scoring."

"Nah, only people fool enough to team up with him don't get to score. We've got nothing to worry about there."

"No one's ever accused this keeper of being able to *keep her*." Enrique's laughing at his own pun messed up the delivery of that line, but his brother offered him a fist to pound anyway.

The ref's whistle called a halt to Dante's roasting, thank the fútbol gods. He didn't even mind, in the end, that his team lost, or the way his cousins hooted at him when he let in a penalty kick. The sun and the camaraderie and the chance to focus on something as casual and normal as sport were a reset he needed. He had barely more than a day before meeting Amalia and their friends for dinner, and he needed to use the time and space to drill into his head that he'd gotten all the practice kissing he was going to get out of her.

⇒⋙ ♥ ⋘⇐

Livia and Greg were already seated when they arrived, nestled into a cozy back booth of the Honey Wine Cafe. Livia's B&B, Chata, adjoined Greg's eco-adventure company, Cesta. Amalia had crafted storefront signs for them both, and Livia placed some of Amalia's for-sale art on her grounds. They'd split some nice commissions, between her guests who bought the pieces at Chata and the ones Livia had referred to Amalia's studio.

After all the hellos, Dante slid into booth first, his bulk

shifting so only his shoulders brushed hers, as they consulted their menus.

"Chicken Fried Steak Night," Greg announced, like any of them didn't have the weekly specials memorized from way back. The owner, Ellie Cerny, added mushroom and fried cauliflower tacos to Tuesday Taco Night back in 2017, and people still referred to that as 'the new menu.'

"And Ellie's a sucker for him, so you know it'll come with extra gravy." Livia had yet to run out of ways to tease her partner for being the town rapscallion and the cafe owner's pseudo-son.

"Well, I am her favorite person in the world."

"Uh-huh," Livia said. "Let me just text Jackson you said that." Jackson, who ran the city dump and was best buds with Mike Moll's Uncle Bill, was also Ellie's gentleman friend.

Greg snatched Livia's phone and tucked it in his pocket. It was a moment of merriment, and Amalia relaxed into the sweetness of it all. She got it, really, why Dante craved something like what Greg and Livia had. She lacked any of those underlying urges she'd quizzed Dante about during their picnic, but she appreciated the happiness her friends seemed to find in each other.

And good for them. Her own happiness arose from other sources.

Speaking of: "Hey, thanks again for that reference letter."

Livia reached across the table to grasp her hands. "Did you get it?"

"I'm on the short list."

They whooped a bit, Greg adding his congrats.

"What did you get? Or nearly get?" Dante asked.

"There's a metalworking expo in Kansas, one of the vendors put out a call for fabricators to work in their booth, showing off how we use their equipment. Liv wrote one of my recs, and I'll know in about a week if I got it."

"That's amazing," Dante said, and it was ridiculous how the warmth of his words both lit her up and settled her down.

He was right, though. She *was* amazing. She drummed her hands on the table. "Yeah, they've never had a rasquache artist before, and I'm excited to show what I can do with offcuts and found objects at the expo. Bring some of that make-do and make-bright spirit to the crowd."

"We're excited for you," Greg said, toasting her with his water glass.

"When is it?" Dante pulled up the site on his phone. "Is this FabConKan? In September?"

"That's it. You've heard of it?"

"Been looking at expos since I got my water supply protection specialist certification. If you get in, want to drive up there together? Or if you're going either way, I could go. I have stay on top of, you know, innovation, skills, and knowledge." He said that last bit like he was reading off the expo's promo page.

"You always have to be the star student." She tapped her shoulder to his upper arm when she said it, laughing at his scowled brows. And then she saw Livia looking between the two of them, all speculation and smirks.

"A road trip, huh? Sounds …" Their dinners arrived, and Livia sat back. "Thanks, Pam."

She dug in without offering further thoughts about what a road trip with Dante sounded like. Her eyes, though, made clear she wasn't expecting it would be strictly a professional jaunt.

Amalia had already had to quash Livia's teasing insinuations about this dinner. It had been Dante's idea to brainstorm with Greg and Livia, who were well-connected with several of the FoundersFest chairs, about the best ways to get her proposal taken seriously at the upcoming planning meeting. Two minutes after he'd set up the group text to pick a time to meet, Amalia was fielding Livia's nosy messages.

She narrowed her eyes at Livia, and shot her a quick text under the table's cover. "Quit acting like this is a double date."

Greg slid Livia's phone out of his pocket, passed it to her, then leaned in to read the message his wife showed him. They snorted practically in unison, the jerks.

Livia and Greg had the kind of connection she'd been thinking about when she asked Dante if the reason he wanted a relationship was for the shared moments together. They weren't smug about it, but it was obvious when she spent time with them. Individually, they were fine people, good friends. As a couple, they took such obvious pleasure in seeing each other engaged by the world, and it kinda amped up their mutual delight. And that was nice for them, even if their giddiness prompted them to believe some fucking wrong ideas about her and Dante.

Who tipped his head towards her to murmur, "Sorry. If that was intrusive of me."

Like his whispering in her ear wouldn't encourage Livia or whoever else might be spying in the Honey Wine Cafe to invent gossip about them. Or like she needed that intimate space between them to conjure up ideas of long hours on the road together, debating playlists and drive-thru choices, stretching at rest stops. Hotel coffee to get them going in the morning. Hotel rooms to retreat to at night.

Casual as anything, when she slid the basket of onion rings to the center of the table, she shifted towards the edge of the booth. It gave her back just a bit of the breathing room she needed to center herself in her own space.

⇾⋙♥⋘⇽

He'd overstepped at dinner.

Maybe she had, too, teasing him about studying, but it

wouldn't have come up if he hadn't invited himself along on her work trip.

In the parking lot after Greg and Livia took off, Dante slumped back against his truck, arms crossed. "I really had been looking for an opportunity like that expo. Shouldn't have just invited myself along, though. Sorry about that. And about turning the talk from what you accomplished, instead of making room to celebrate you."

She propped up against her own pickup and gave him a look that seemed to scan him for sincerity. "Appreciate the apology. And that you figured out on your own that you were stealing focus—even though you noticed it too late to stop yourself."

"Yeah. I'll ... do some work on that."

"Good. And, hey, I'm not saying no to Kansas, if it suits our schedules. But maybe don't go broadcasting that in front of some of the nosiest people in town."

"More smart advice." He shoved his hands in his pockets, to stop himself from getting fidgety. "I ought to know better about gossip around here."

"Yeah, you ought to. I already got a text from Patti asking if we were together."

"Shit, seriously?"

She flashed him her phone screen, which overflowed with suggestive emojis.

Dante groaned.

"It's fine. I'll set her straight. I should have known us showing up at the cafe with another couple would mean tongues wagging."

Another couple. He suddenly wasn't so paranoid about her being annoyed with him.

Amalia finished messaging Patti. "She confirmed she's coming to the meeting on Thursday."

"Nice, more strength in numbers. And you heard Greg and Ellie are meeting up Tuesday to talk to Jackson? I think we're on our way to critical mass. Mike's going to have to pay attention."

Amalia's smile was small but true. "In theory, anyway. I'm more hopeful than I was before you started talking me up."

He was sure his expression revealed how much he appreciated her saying so. He cleared his throat. "I've been doing more homework. Independent study this time. Your rasquache stuff? I didn't know what to call it before."

"Mike calls it chaos."

"Well, fuck Mike. I know Honey Wine has plenty of room to show off how the borderlands have always been part of who we are. Like you said about different traditions of folk art all contributing to our culture."

Maybe it was the moonlight, maybe wishful thoughts, but he didn't know that he'd seen such a soft expression on Amalia before. "You've been paying attention, star student."

"Got to know enough to prove your right to participate to everyone. Speaking of, you know Jorge's neighbors at all, down the back of his property?"

"Not to speak to." When she shook her head, a wisp of her hair went flying off in the breeze.

He kept his hands to himself. "You might ask him about them, if we get our way. They do this basket-making. Weaving. Natural materials they cultivate and gather. Not the whole family, but the craft's been handed down across generations. Could be interesting."

"Nice. I'll hit him up." She stepped up into her truck, offering a wave he took as his cue to head home himself.

Dante followed her out of town, a trail of taillights leading him into the dark, his mind still caught on that soft smile. And on the rightness of all the reasons he'd gone to Amalia for help in the first place. Because he was lucky enough to count her a friend. Because her explanation of how yoga would help him with the physical toll of being a plumber had been matter-of-fact, and clear, and absolutely correct. Because he'd never caught wind of her gossiping. Because her brains and her talent and her attitude broadcast to everyone that she was one of those destined for greatness, which put her firmly out of his reach.

The more fool him, going into it sure he could keep his feelings to himself. Confident his awe of her would mean it was safe, somehow, to let her see all his flaws. He'd never be good enough, but damn it all to hell if he didn't keep remembering that smile.

And fuck if he didn't also remember her warning against looking for a wife who would broadcast his status. The risk of using a partner as a way to prove to the world that he was worthy. He'd seen it plenty, in culture and in life, those preening men, cock-of-the-walk that their women were hot stuff. Acting like her desirability was proof that he'd won some masculinity contest.

Their trucks rumbled across the bridge over the Blanco. Dante braked a bit, in anticipation of Amalia turning off towards her place. She disappeared from his sight, while he carried on, determined to fight off the impulse to worship her.

CHAPTER 11

The town's meeting room didn't exactly overflow with people coming to plan FoundersFest. Mr. Connor presided over the podium, as always when there was a chance for him to feel a touch of power. Mike Moll, of course, and a few of the other crafts-and-antiques type store owners. Ellie from the cafe, sandwiched between Jackson and Bill, the old guys who spent much of their days gossiping while pretending not to be the main movers of the Honey Wine grapevine. Greg and Livia. A few of the other local artists—Patti, Jorge, Nicole.

And quietly beside her, somehow using his height and strength as a bulwark she'd never expected at her side, Dante.

He leaned toward her as Mr. Connor cleared his throat. "Feeling optimistic?" His low voice arrowed straight into her ear, despite the buzzing room.

Before she could answer, Mr. Connor tapped the microphone. "All right, all right, no need to chat the whole evening away. Are the committee heads ready to update everyone for this year's FoundersFest?"

Ellie stood and moved towards the podium, only to shake her head and plunk herself back down when Mike Moll spoke up from his seat.

"We need to keep in mind the ethos of FoundersFest. Yes, we want to highlight our authentic small-town vibe, not fill a bunch of booths with commercial junk. But FoundersFest is about celebrating the history of Honey Wine. The Czech settlers who traveled here after the 1848 Revolutions, and gave our town the character that's so appealing to tourists. Look how Chata and Cesta are taking off, trading on that heritage. And Ellie's Czech-inspired dishes being such a draw at the cafe. You can hardly find seating on Goulash Night. So that's what I'm cultivating for the Art Walk—authenticity and tradition. I've approved several artists already, and I'm taking applications to review for the remaining booths."

Amalia traded looks with Livia, who elbowed Greg, who turned around to murmur at Ellie. She turned to Jackson, tugging him down by the sleeve so she could make what looked like an emphatic point. Jackson leant over her head to furrow his impressive brows at Mike's Uncle Bill. Bill shrugged a little, but hinged forward to the row ahead to listen to whatever Greg had to tell him. It wouldn't be everything she'd told her friends about Mike's agenda, but any bit of a wedge helped open the door for her.

Mr. Connor raised his hands, performing the illusion he wasn't already losing control of the meeting. "Okay, Mike," he said, dry as usual. "We'll circle back to that when the agenda calls for the Art Walk Committee report. Ellie, can you—"

Ellie moved more quickly this time, that hummingbird quality of hers coming into play as she bypassed Mike Moll and edged Frank Connor away from the podium. Her report on the food vendors was thorough and unusually brief, for anyone speaking to the town. "And this year, we're adding a chili cook-off as well as the usual kolache contest. I've got Pam and Maria coming up with a judging panel for the chili, and Livia's taking over Kent's spot to judge the kolaches."

"And hoping the winners will agree to supply me for my

guests," Livia said, rubbing her hands together like she was an evil mastermind, and not someone devoted to giving every visitor to Honey Wine a memorable experience.

Mr. Connor jotted something down, then took back his podium. Dante's pals in logistics reported on equipment rentals and layout, swearing they'd provided for more shaded seating than the year before. Mr. Connor confirmed he'd pushed through all the permits. Jackson Apel went over the budget, whipping up enough yes votes to approve some additional advertising.

"Ought to get some of our artists to design the ads," Bill called out.

Mike nodded. "How about it, Nicole? You got time?"

What Nicole had was a two-year-old daughter, part-time college classes, and a full-time job, in addition to the prints she made as her side-hustle. It amazed Amalia that she'd managed the time to show up to the meeting. It did not amaze Amalia that Mike didn't seem to consider any of that when instead he could assign a woman to do unpaid work.

Nicole looked at Mike, head tilted, lips pursed. "I could maybe find some. Send me the specs and I'll let y'all know."

"And since Mike presented early, I see that completes our committee reports," Mr. Connor said, looking around the room. "Any other business?"

Dante shifted beside Amalia, unfolding with greater speed than his usual, as he stood to face the room. "I've got something."

Heads turned, maybe in surprise, given Dante's quiet way of moving through the community. Mr. Connor simply made room at the podium.

"So, Mike talked about the Forty Eighters, and that's truly something. All the work people did, coming over here from Bohemia, creating community and fighting for abolition and giving us kolaches to eat."

The people around her softened, attentive.

"But like I told Mike last week, this event is called FoundersFest. We know how important tradition is around here. But it's broader than just the Bohemian side we've celebrated other years. There's more history to celebrate, and it's getting ignored."

"And like I told you, that's great and all, but it's not why people come to FoundersFest." Mike's glare moved from Dante over to Amalia. "No matter what people keep claiming when they're out to advance their own personal agendas."

Ellie turned on him. "Now, if that were the strict truth, I'd not have the enthusiasm from all my chili chefs."

"Well, who doesn't like chili?"

"Not my point, Mike. Everyone likes pizza, too, but we're not setting up a bunch of brick ovens. Chili con carne is part of our state's deep Tejano roots, and that goes back to before a single handful of Czech people set foot in the Hill Country. And that's why we added the cook-off to FoundersFest this year. I'm looking to add some Tex-Mex booths to the food hall, too."

Dante crossed his arms. "Ellie's saying what I mean. About Tejano and Mexican American culture. We all love Honey Wine, but you can't erase us from its history."

Mike flushed red. "Hang on, it's not racist to keep the focus on what's always made the festival a success. Tourists like the Bohemian angle."

Bill fixed his nephew with one of those familial looks that promised a talking-to if Mike didn't hush.

Mr. Connor stood shoulder-to-shoulder with Dante. "I like it. This idea of including our whole heritage. Thoughts?"

Amalia felt Greg's double-take, but Greg never did get past the negative impressions he and Mr. Connor had made on each other when Greg was a teen.

Patti lifted a hand. "Some of the players in my brother's polka band also do Norteño music. That's a direct link between different sides of who settled around here."

Jorge belted out, "¡Voy desvelado!" Before everyone could join in the chorus, Mr. Connor clapped, once, into the mic.

"I'm sensing enthusiasm. Ellie, I'll leave it to you, but you should ask Cypress who has that taco truck that operated out of his parking lot last Sunday. The smoked lamb was astounding. And it seems Mike has room in the Art Walk to expand. Patti, pass your brother's info on to Bob—oh, you've got it?" He nodded at Bob's affirmative chin jerk. "Nicole, you'll want to hold off on developing more graphics until we have a clearer idea of our direction, but let me know your availability. Hmm. The dance exhibition, we'll want to see about expanding that. And find more space in the craft tents. The games tent, I don't know. Does anyone have ideas there?"

"We could have Lotería," Amalia said.

"And dominoes," added someone from the back of the room. She turned to see who—it was Mrs. Connor—and caught sight of Dante. He'd faded to the back wall of the room. She couldn't quite credit how he'd said three or four sentences, and broken through where none of the researched presentations she'd been lobbing at Mike Moll had.

The power of being well-liked. Or of being a tall, handsome man. Or of people worried they'd not get Dante to their houses in a plumbing emergency. Or of the quiet groundwork he'd been successful at laying for the past few weeks. Or all of it. Fucking frustrating, was what it was, but it reinforced that her asking Dante for help had been a smart move on her part.

They wrapped up, after Mr. Connor emphasized his reporting deadlines. Mike shoved back his chair. "Glad we've spent so much time working towards plans that might have to go and change now."

A few mutters—and a few louder voices—took care to chime in with dissent, now it was off the record. "Is anyone going to check with the sponsors?" "Seems like we could stick to the familiar this year and ease into big changes for next time." "Is this even gonna get an official vote?"

Bob, owner of Bob's Bar, which anchored one corner of the town square, cleared his throat and narrowed his eyes. "Y'all need to stop getting all bent out of shape. Lad's had a good idea, can't be that much harm in it. We book some new bands, sell some different food. Easy peasy."

Greg snorted a laugh, but that was more of his residual conviction that Mr. Connor would obstruct all progress. Livia covered with a grin. "Well said. Let's go drink to that."

Dante strolled a few minutes late into Bob's Bar—no one seemed surprised he'd stayed behind to help Frank Connor re-stack the chairs. His friends had pushed a couple tables together. Amalia scooted a chair in his direction. "Got us shots to celebrate your success."

He shook his head. "Just told them all what you told me."

"Well, it worked. And it never worked when I was the one saying it."

He pretty much despised the truth of that. Someone as bright and talented as Amalia was someone who ought to find it easy to be heard. "I feel wrong-footed. I expected more push-back, not just that muttering at the end there. Been running all these 'if this happens then we try that' scenarios for days, and instead it seems like we might have turned the tide your way already."

The others looked to agree. Jorge was reprising his performance of "Desvelado," sweeping half the table up into the chorus, though not a one of them could hold a candle to Bobby Pulido.

Dante and Amalia downed their shots. After a bit of listening, of watching friends banter back and forth, of feeling warm in the midst of cheer, he ventured up to get the next round.

Waiting on Bob to fill the glasses, he turned and caught

Amalia's eye. The others were absorbed in whatever and nonsense, but something in the way she looked at him caught him up still. There were ideas lurking in her head, and he was curious to hear about them. What else could they do, to push along the expansion of FoundersFest? Had she come up with some new and maybe devious scheme to out-maneuver Mike Moll? Was there something major he'd missed and she was thinking how to break the news to him?

When she cornered him, a beer or so in, he ought not to have been surprised. But dancing eyes and elbow nudge or no, he wasn't expecting, "We need you to go on a date."

Dante did not choke. He shook his head, but she nodded, all loose enthusiasm.

"No listen. I'll set you up, or if you have a pick, that's fine. Look." She pointed to a few tables off to the side, and then up to the bar. "You meet someone there, and I can take one of the barstools, and watch you in the mirror. I can tell you afterwards where you go wrong."

"Fuck no."

"Come on."

"Sounds like torture. Especially if you'd going into it expecting me to go wrong."

"You're the one …" Amalia shot a look around the table, then lowered her voice. "The one who asked for help. We haven't figured anything else new by keeping it between the two of us. I need to see what you're doing, if my feedback is going to be of any use."

"Yeah, no."

"Dante, come on. It makes sense. This doesn't need to be someone you're convinced will be your wife one day—unless, by some good fortune, she will. But you have to take it as for real, so I can figure out solutions."

He took time draining his glass. "How are you serious about this?"

"How are you putting up resistance? You want to fix your

dating life, find a partner you like pleasing. Great sex starts with great communication which means trying for great dates."

The dim bar lights probably hid any blushing he was doing. And maybe, if he agreed, her watching him attempt to charm someone, between the low light and the murky mirror, wouldn't reveal every one of his inadequacies. Only the ones he was still hoping she'd help him correct.

"Fine." He softened his own voice, cause he didn't need anyone there guessing at the methods he was trying to overcome his reputation. "One date."

And if it felt all kinds of wrong to submit to this plan, well, that was also no one's business. Not even Amalia's.

CHAPTER 12

Amalia: I noticed you still haven't answered my question

Dante: You ask a lot of questions

Amalia: yeah, but only one of them brings up NSFW terms

Dante thunked the jar of peanut butter on his kitchen table so he could type with both hands.

Dante: I thought you were going to throw more date options at me. Not whatever this is

Amalia: This is me hoping that you'll tell me your porn habits if you can hide behind a screen while you finally spill

Amalia: your search terms. Spill your search terms. Nothing else.

Dante: hilarious

> Amalia: go on, then. MILFs? Threesomes? Bondage? I understand hentai is popular. IDK why, but your thing for detective novels seems to match up with that.

> Dante: your mind is a mysterious place

> Amalia: Well, it's not like I think you search for Miss Marple smut.

He phoned her. "Miss Marple?"

She kept laughing as he repeated his question.

"No, but seriously, you're ridiculous. I want that on some kind of official record."

She hummed. "The official record of your PornHub account."

"Amalia." He went back to mixing the peanut-ginger marinade. "I already told you, porn hasn't taught me anything about how to be good at sex myself."

"But you get off with it?"

"Obviously. I'm really skilled at masturbating. Are you recording this conversation?"

"If only. Okay, answer the door."

He glanced at his now-silent cell, then at the front of the house. Sure enough, a knock, and there she was. Carrying bags of take-out and smirking like she'd bested him somehow.

Probably she had. He sighed and led her to the kitchen, where he set about putting away his stir-fry prep.

"That looks good. Are you a decent cook?"

"Yep. Been feeding myself ever day for a long time now."

She hip-bumped him aside to make room for herself and began to unpack her bags. "I see I got your hackles nice and raised. I figured you'd keep putting up resistance, so I'm buttering you up with eggplant parm and confiscating your phone."

He slid his phone from his back pocket and set it in the shelves above the fridge. "Nope."

"Don't you play tall games with me, Dante Morales. We are eating messy pasta and watching nude people do things to each other. Unless solo play is your preference. You know I don't judge."

"No, you only snoop." He dried his hands and set out plates. "We don't need to do this, Amalia. I did that metaphorical garden work. I identified that my go-tos are women riding men. And blow jobs, of course. I'm in touch with my desires."

She pointed a spatula at him. "Ha. I knew if I pestered you in enough ways you'd fess up."

He wiped up the marinara she'd dripped on the counter. "Yeah, well. I'm not giving you my phone."

She set the plates at his table, positioning them side-by-side, instead of where they'd be across from one another while they ate. "Come on."

Dante was still suspicious, but he grabbed a couple of beers and joined her. "Thanks for dinner."

"Thanks for letting me in. Look, I know I've stayed on this, but there's a reason. You've got these overlapping factors. One is how you—I don't know if you've been selfish in bed, or if you were just bad at cluing in to your partner, but either way it got you using sex to get just yourself off. And the other is how now you're self-conscious about your performance and how that impacts your confidence. And your communication."

The pasta was tasty. The eggplant was a little soggy, which was no surprise after time in the takeout container. He ate it anyway. And then he looked at Amalia. "I'm aware."

"You're mad at me."

"Hmm. Maybe." Dante set down his utensils. "I think I feel ... pushed. And I know I asked for it, so I need to get over it, but between the porn questions, and your idea I have to go on a date, it's all very uncomfortable for me right now."

Amalia bit her lips, nodding. "Okay. That's understandable."

"So you'll drop it?"

She studied him and seemed to guess he was overacting his relief. He'd told the truth about his discomfort, but he also always felt pretty at easy around Amalia, which made things better.

Instead of giving him a break, she took out her own phone. "Already got private browsing set up. I'd guessed some reverse cowgirl would suit you, how insightful am I?"

He slumped. "Amalia."

"Relax. It's barely two minutes." She leant the phone against her longneck, and pressed play. "But we can watch more after this if you want."

He shook his head, but also adjusted the phone's angle to see better. Amalia's next bite of eggplant seemed smug, somehow, but whatever. He would watch the nice people fuck, and then this exercise would be over.

Amalia slurped up some pasta and made loud mmmmmmmm noises. Smacked her lips. "So good, right?"

"Hold up. Did you get us eggplant parm because of the eggplants? You're a real ass sometimes," he muttered, and very carefully did not shift in his seat to better shield his impending erection.

"Speaking of peachy asses, look at hers bounce. Don't you just want to grab it?"

"Shut up, Amalia."

"Okay, I will. If you tell me why you think she's arching her back. What does that mean?"

"It means you have weird ideas about teaching. And also that she probably wants someone to grab her tits."

"Could be." She patted his shoulder and he refused to

flinch. "Could be she's tilting her pelvis to get a better angle for his dick at her g-spot."

Dante gripped the edge of his chair. Maybe she was laughing at how out of control this was making him, but fuck if, between her goading and the scene, he didn't want to start talking more. "I—if she was on my dick, I'd have to listen to, to her moans and all. Since I can't see her face. Maybe I can tell from the way she digs her nails into my thighs."

"Uh-huh. That's good. I like how you observed that." Her voice was low and husky and he wanted to watch the words leave her mouth. But he also refused to look away from her phone screen. "You can also ask her."

"Ask her." He wasn't sure if he was asking Amalia, or just repeating.

"Yeah. Ask if it feels good. If you're fucking her at a nice angle. If she wants you to rub her clit."

"No one's rubbing her clit now." He gulped. "Poor clit. He should be doing that."

"Oh, he absolutely should. Or she could do it herself. Look how she's letting him take over thrusting from below. Look how he isn't touching her pussy at all, and now he's going to come and she's just ..."

"Just letting him. And he's not even grabbing her tits. He doesn't care about anything but his own pleasure. Selfish."

"Mmm, no. I think you're right. I'm so glad that's not going to be you anymore. You should be proud of all the work you're up to. Okay, show's over, good night."

Amalia snatched up her phone and waltzed out of his house. Dante didn't even stop to lock it behind her before he shoved back his chair, pulled out his aching cock, and came with the echo of her teasing hums in his head.

⇢⋙♥⋘⇠

Dante kept rejecting all of Amalia's suggestions for him to take on the bar date. Susanna was too hung up on Lynne. Lynne was too young. Kylie turned him down last year. Fern, he didn't bother to say why he wouldn't date her, just: no. Her best guess, based on Fern and Kylie having a lot in common, was that Fern was too much a person he'd want to be in a real relationship with, so he wouldn't approach her until he was over his issues.

By the time he agreed to ask out Natasha, she'd spent an unfathomable amount of time—okay, six days—considering Dante's taste in women.

At least she'd finally pushed him into the porn conversation, so she never had to think about Dante's tastes there anymore. Or about the way his cheekbones flushed when he was talking about it, or about how very still he'd held himself, so good and restrained as he answered her questions.

She'd definitively crossed that item off their teach Dante about fucking plan.

Showing up at Bob's that Friday, shedding her raincoat and shaking her hair out of its clip, she headed straight for one of the few remaining barstools. The damp of a particularly heavy late spring rain hovered in her bones long enough for her to consider liquor instead of the beer she'd intended.

Except she needed to stay sharp if this spy-on-a-date plan wasn't going to be a waste of her time. Once she had her longneck, she double-checked that Dante and Natasha hadn't yet shown. They weren't at the tables she could see from the bar mirror, nor could she spot them once she swiveled to investigate.

She'd just swiveled back to the bar when they walked in and huddled in the doorway under Dante's umbrella. Natasha had a grip on Dante's arm, clearly in the midst of a dramatic tale. Amalia tilted the beer bottle, and when she clocked them again, she was confronted with Dante's date clothes. Jeans, but new-looking, a tucked-in button-down, even a belt. But also his work boots, mud-splattered as if to justify their place on this date.

She glanced at Natasha's feet; her flats were leaving wet prints behind as they approached the bar. She was laughing, though, and saying, "Isn't it ridiculous?"

Dante made the briefest of eye contact with Amalia before nodding and hanging his and Natasha's gear on the crowded wall hooks.

Natasha went on about an argument she'd had with a coworker, and Dante leaned down to listen, a hand between Natasha's shoulder blades as he guided her towards one of the tables Amalia had suggested.

"But maybe he'll cave," Dante said.

Natasha shook her head as they passed through the last of Amalia's mirror-blind-spots. "You obviously don't know my credit manager."

"I, no. I don't know him," he said, or she thought he did. Either way, in the mirror, she saw them settle in and do that thing where they both had forearms on the table. Her butt was almost off the chair as they tilted towards an intimate space together.

So far, so good, with the spying. No notes. Dante had body language and attentive listening down pat. Maybe things with Natasha would work out great, and all the time Amalia spent fixing a man would pay off for the two of them.

Bob distracted her asking if she wanted another beer. She switched to soda, since she'd already blamed the alcohol for the snaky feeling of dismay she was wrestling with. It wasn't one of those nice snaky feelings, either, the kind she could pin on someone else's bad behavior. This slithering was all from her own regret at having inflicted the situation on herself.

Natasha and Dante were still hunched conspiratorially across the table almost an hour later, when she saw him pull his phone from his pocket. He said something brief, and

Natasha nodded as Dante retreated down the restroom corridor.

Amalia followed his progress in the mirror, meeting his gaze as he returned to the main room. He paused by her stool and said, "I just heard from Public Works. The Blanco is rising, and they called me in to check on some storm drains. Will you let Bob know, so he can send people home if they have to cross it?"

"Yeah, of course. What else?"

"Can you give Natasha a ride home?"

By the time Amalia made it to Dante's table, Natasha had caught wind of the flood alert and arranged for a departing neighbor to drop her off.

"Give me a call tomorrow," Natasha said. "If you're not too waterlogged."

Maybe it turned out Dante's type was someone unbothered by him ditching her on a moment's notice.

He shuffled a bit and said, "Yeah, of course, I'll try."

He held her raincoat for her, but made no move to walk her to the door.

After Natasha's departure, Amalia side-eyed Dante, "We'll talk about all that. Later."

His face. It would be nice of her to cut him a break, but much more fun not to.

Dante shook it all off and donned his own coat. Amalia grabbed her stuff and followed him out. "So what's the plan? Where do they need us?"

"You're coming with?"

"You thought I'd leave you and everyone to deal with it?" She stopped to fish her cowboy boots, ball cap, and a spare shirt from her truck.

He shook his head, but held the door while she set herself up in his pickup. Fortunately they'd both parked close enough to the door to avoid Bob's more pitted and now-soggy spaces. "It's going to be a mess. Gross. Wet. Maybe stinky."

"I know. Not my first flood." For most of its history, Honey Wine had weathered storm events okay, but between climate change and the growth of the town, they'd learned to expect problems.

"If we're lucky, it won't come to that. Rain's meant to stop by three in the morning, but County says they've got trees in the river just upstream of the Clay Road turnoff, so I'm going to start there."

Fun times. She texted some friends along RR12, in case they weren't getting other alerts. The rain drummed on the cab roof, the headlights refracted around the falling drops, the wipers swished in high gear. As Dante rounded the corner onto Cypress Ridge, Amalia shook off her mesmerization. "You have whatever equipment you need with you?"

He flexed his hands on the steering wheel. "Hmm. I have lights and PPE in the side box, and curb keys, plus the winch if that's necessary. Probably it won't be; Public Works is better equipped for that, but my contract lets me use it if I can't get them in place instead. If I need snakes or to install a backwater valve, I'll have to head back for my van, but all that's going to be more of a tomorrow problem."

The drains he checked were clear. He let the third metal cover drop back into place and pushed himself to standing. "Heard anything new?"

Amalia adjusted the flashlight to guide them back to the truck. "Honey Creek is over its banks, but not threatening anyone so far."

"Your boots holding up?"

They'd bickered a bit about her footwear, but she was comfortable with how they'd suit her climbing on slippy embankments and navigating dirty puddles. And they kept her toes drier than her tennis shoes would have. "Stop fretting. There more drains to inspect this direction?"

"Nah, if we've not heard of blockage yet, the rest of this

run should hold. Better to check in on the downed trees and see if I can help there. Want me to drop you back to your place, or to Bob's?"

"What part of me coming with didn't you understand? No wonder you didn't pick up on Natasha looking for a goodnight kiss, if it's so easy for you to stop paying attention to people."

"Natasha wanted a kiss?"

She tucked the heavy-duty flashlight into the door pocket. "Or a hug, or a 'gee, it sucks our date was cut short,' or any kind of indication you weren't in a rush to be done with her."

All he said to that was, "Huh." But his grip on the steering wheel stayed tight as they headed back to the river.

A couple miles out, the county truck was parked across the road, emergency lights flashing. Dante rolled down his window enough to get the news from the guys in reflective vests.

"The retention areas on those new builds along Honey Creek overflowed—no storm drains there yet. So the creek is filling with junk, and we've got to pull back to see what we can do about the low-water crossings on RR12."

Dante's shoulders sank. "You think it's going to get enough water on the street side to hit homes?"

"That's where we're headed," another rain-slickered guy said. "We've got Felder's guys to the east; they'll check those trees when it's light."

"Let us know. We'll head back to Bob's and work on sandbagging the square."

"Good man. Thanks."

Rain mostly obscured the mountain laurels lining the road, but she caught glimpses of them waving erratically in Dante's headlights, as he turned the truck towards town. He was shooting her indecipherable looks, but it wasn't until he was driving on the comparatively high surfaces of Cypress Ridge that he said, "What if I didn't want to kiss her?"

CHAPTER 13

Amalia didn't answer right away. It wasn't much like her, to not have opinions.

"I know you had to dig at me to ask her on a date. I appreciate all that, not sure if I said so earlier." Problem was, asking out Natasha didn't change that he was struggling to not be hung up on Amalia.

He'd always been attracted to Amalia, even back when he was a freshman and she the coolest senior at the high school. And then they'd gone separate ways a bit, and recently they'd come back together as friends, and even more recently he'd pushed himself to ask if she'd be interested in grabbing a meal with him. Once she'd turned him down, he'd thought that could be it. The end of a high school infatuation, the blooming of a solid friendship. A trajectory common as limestone, if equally crushing when set atop his romantic feelings.

Turned out, he'd been fooling himself. Once he started talking more intimately with Amalia, the groundwater of his feelings went and eroded the limestone, and now they were bubbling up all over the place.

The best solution he'd come up with was to put a halt to their whole deal. He was holding off, wary that Amalia would refuse his help with the Art Walk if he told her he was done with his lessons.

"You didn't," she said. Or maybe asked.

In the rain-darkened intimacy of the truck, he pushed himself to clarify. "I didn't tell you thanks, or I didn't want to kiss Natasha?"

"Well, I know for sure about the first. Not about the second. And obviously you don't have to kiss anyone you don't want to. The point of the date was for us to see how you acted in it, not to force you to follow any kind of script."

He slowed for a turn. Glanced at her. "Except the script of being in the moment. I think I did that, you know. Talking with her didn't set off any landmines like I did with Jules, or whoever. I didn't even tell her to prepare her womb to bear my children."

She covered her mouth, but her guffaw escaped. "Fucking hell, Dante."

"Too far?" He grinned.

"In Texas, under this administration? I sure as shit think so."

"See? You agree I'm getting so much better at casual conversation." He sighed. "For real, though, the social part did feel better. I don't know if it would be the same if ..."

Rain pattered on the roof, then drummed louder, drowning out whatever he might have confessed. The road glistened under the deepening storm, wipers barely keeping up with the torrents pelting the windshield. He was grateful for his relatively new tires.

"Hanging in there?" Amalia leaned in to speak over the outside noise. "Are you still okay to drive?"

He forced his shoulders down. "Just need to take it slow. Be on Main in a minute." She knew the roads as well as he did, even with the crap visibility. It helped to talk through his tension, though. He eased off the gas, peering through sheeting water.

Maybe Amalia needed to chatter away nerves, too. She said, "I could use a cup of coffee."

He nodded. "Hope Bob put some on. Even if it's that caramel one he likes so much."

"Ick."

"Right?"

His headlights pierced the rain, revealing figures huddled against the storm. Parked vehicles lined the square, lights reflecting off the slick street and heaped sandbags. Dante pulled into a spot, and they dashed through puddles to the overhang where a pallet of bags and pile of flood barriers waited.

Bob boomed greetings over the chaos. "River's coming up fast! Y'all got gloves?"

Dante did; Amalia stopped at her truck for a pair that fit her smaller hands. Soon enough they caught the rhythm of the line, passing bags into position. Digging trenches where needed. Filling in the gaps when people dipped out for a break—Bob turned coffee duty over to Ellie when she showed up. Moving vehicles to shine headlights on areas under threat. Heads down, bodies in constant motion, adrenaline beating back exhaustion, the necessity of working together blunting whatever interpersonal differences people might harbor on sunnier days.

Honey Wine had learned through trial, error, and the bitter experience of being located close to a high water table, to move fast as soon as the banks overspilled at Creekside Park, or risk damage to many of the places essential to their economy. No one wanted to mar the charm of the town with a lot of concrete infrastructure, but funds for greener infrastructure kept getting diverted to more urgent problems. Or problems the people who weren't spending all night on flood watch deemed more urgent.

A couple hours of bagging—could have been three—and Dante couldn't remember what dry felt like. He shoved soaked hair from his eyes and caught sight of Amalia heading into the welcoming light of the cafe. The mud sucked at his boots, but he kept his footing as he squelched after her.

It was almost too bright to figure things out, once he was inside. The quiet murmur of exhausted voices was an assault after the torrents of rainfall.

Jackson handed him a shop towel, only slightly grimy, but almost entirely dry. "Give me your coat, I'll hang it with the rest. Want to leave your boots there?"

He followed the man's guidance to a tarp piled with filthy footwear. "Thanks."

"Sure thing. Grab a seat, someone'll be by with a sandwich."

Dante didn't exactly plan it out, but whatever force was at work on him landed him in Amalia's booth. When he'd downed a glass of water and blinked himself to alertness, he lifted a weary hand. "Heya."

She grunted in reply.

"Yep."

Pam slid coffee cups onto the table. "Ham or cheese or both?"

"Both, thanks." Amalia wrapped her hands around her mug as soon as it was full.

"Same. Thanks, Pam."

"Thanks to you both. Looks like we're turning a corner out there."

If so, Dante was glad. He'd left his phone in his truck, and was too much in the middle of things for any kind of overview of the situation. "Anyone heard from Greg?"

"They're fine, but Forst Creek is high, too. They might lose the bridge."

"Damn."

Pam patted his shoulder before heading to the next group of volunteers. Dante turned to Amalia, who hadn't moved to un-bag her sandwich. Her eyes were closed. He set both their sandwiches out on napkins and added cream to their coffees. She still didn't move, and he let loose a tired smile as he propped his feet on the opposite bench and wrapped an arm around Amalia.

She muttered, but settled against his chest. Holding her, forcing his muscles to relax into as much of a cushion as he could offer her, he just ... watched her rest. Let himself close his own eyes for a moment and press his nose into her damp hair. Sniffed the crown of her head, but only lightly, because the blurriness of exhaustion wouldn't close anyone's prying eyes.

By the time he was half through his coffee, she'd roused enough to start on her sandwich, still tucked into him. They ate as voices swirled around them; mutters about the power holding, and emergency services being overwhelmed, and how this was worse than May Day 2014 or summer '98 or, rumor had it, even 1921.

When the food was gone and the coffee cold, Amalia shifted. "We should get back out there."

"Yeah." He couldn't bring himself to let her go before she made to move. "We probably should."

Ellie foisted cookies on them as they reapplied their mucky outer layers. Dante offered his to Bob when they got back to command central. The square was still full of volunteers, including heavy equipment someone had brought in. The air in the overhang stank of mud and fuel. Since no one had—so far—sought him out to deal with sewage backups or broken pipes, he didn't bother to mind the stench.

Flashlights and headlights revealed water beginning to rise into low-lying sections despite their efforts. Amalia headed over to help lay tarps where a line needed reshaping. Bill was ready for a break, so Dante hopped into the forklift to move pallets in easier reach of the danger zones.

Inside the enclosed cabin of the rough terrain forklift, Dante didn't notice when the rain finally moved off. He was only existing in the needs of the moment. It was the kind of alert but disconnected way he'd felt talking to Natasha. He could focus on the exact sentence she was saying, but not the overall thrust of the conversation. Like moving a pallet from point A to point B without a single thought to the endpoint of the work, because he'd surrendered to the need to just get the job done. It took until he saw someone's pickup bed draped with a collection of coats and flannels for him to register that the sky was clearing with the first cloudy hints of dawn.

Thank *fuck*.

He maneuvered to a clear stretch of pavement and stepped out to gauge how Honey Wine looked.

It could have been much worse. Sandbags held at critical spots, though some lines were down to two skinny bags and sheer luck. Others had been cleared in places to shore up elsewhere, leaving loose tarps to whip in the wind. Dozens of pallets littered the perimeter of their defense. A few cars sank into the storm-soaked verge, probably abandoned until the ground dried up some.

He couldn't spot Amalia.

By the time he'd corralled the empty pallets into Bob's parking lot, a timid rim of grey light lined the eastern sky. He shut down the lift and approached Amalia's truck. She was nowhere near it, but it was as far as he could manage, just then, to move himself. He lowered her tailgate and eased himself to sitting on it.

Everyone looked just as beat as he felt. With a groan, he laid back into the bed of the truck, ignoring the few undrained drops of rain. He could hardly get much wetter, and if history held true, he'd be plenty swamped over the next few days as people discovered broken pipes and faulty sump pumps and back flow preventers that did not, in fact, prevent back flow.

God, he needed sleep.

He didn't want to leave without checking in with Amalia. But. Damn.

CHAPTER 14

She'd zoned out inside the cafe, only blinking herself to awareness when Ellie sat a stack of pancakes in front of her. "Honey or syrup?"

"You are a certified angel."

"Yep, I know."

"Honey, please."

Ellie fetched a jar of honey and a side plate of bacon. Amalia sent her a tired, grateful smile and dug in. It wasn't yet six in the morning, but the Honey Wine Cafe bustled with an almost-usual kind of activity. The entrance needed some serious mopping, and most everyone, staff and patrons, drooped. It was like a bunch of people from a Diego Rivera mural filling up an Edward Hopper diner.

Sweet honey, crunchy bacon, and hot coffee. It was the reviving fuel she needed to propel her out in search of her abandoned coat and gloves and truck. She dropped some cash in the tip jar and lifted her hand in a wave, wishing everyone safe journeys home, and went out in the detritus of Honey Wine's damp early morning.

The gloves were in her jacket pockets. The jacket was draped on the bench she'd been passing when the rain finally stopped. Her truck ... right. It was still in Bob's parking lot, because in the prehistory of ten hours earlier, she'd been spying on Dante's date.

Some of her stuff was still in Dante's truck, but that was a problem for way off in the future. After a dozen hours of sleep and, oh yeah, anything she might have to do in her own yard after the rains.

It wasn't until she was behind the wheel and noticed the humps of his bent knees in the rearview mirror that she realized she'd found Dante.

He didn't stir at the clang of her closing door. Probably she could drive off with him and he'd stay fast asleep. His face was tilted into the shadow cast by the sidewall, but what sun there was caught and tangled in the dark waves of his hair.

She clambered in beside him, dropping onto her elbow, and poked his shoulder.

"Hey ..." Dante blinked up at her like a dazed cat.

"Morning," Amalia said. "You alive still?"

He scooted into a slightly more alert pose.

"Didn't want to bail without checking on you," he mumbled.

Amalia poked him again to stop herself from going gooey at the idea of him delaying searching out his own bed, in order to see if she'd held up okay. "You could have just texted."

He grunted.

If his eyes had been open, she'd have given him more hell. Also if her own limbs weren't threatening to seize up completely rather than let her maneuver her way back into the driver's seat. "You want to just curl up where you are and I'll drive you home?"

He grunted again, this time in a more negating kind of way.

"No need." His voice cracked like dry wood. "I'm good."

"Good? You're still snoring."

"Don't snore." He scrubbed a hand over his face and blinked hard.

Amalia eyed him skeptically, watching those half-open eyes try to focus. "You shouldn't—"

"It's fine," he insisted, sliding out of the truck. His movements had that stiff fluidity that came with too little sleep and too much resolve.

"If you say so." Amalia fished for her keys with an exasperated sigh. "I'm following you."

He waved his hand in loose dismissal, but she caught sight of him checking the side mirror more than once as they drove through town.

Rainwater dripped from trees and collected in vast muddy puddles. A misty grayness dulled the morning light, giving the streets a quiet, worn-out look. She trailed him at a cautious distance, ready to hit the horn if his truck swerved even a little. Probably her vigilance helped her stay alert, too. It wasn't as if she'd taken even the shortest of naps, and they'd both worked flat-out all night.

When she turned toward her own home at last, exhaustion hit her like a stone. Amalia drove the circuit of her workshop and house before heading in, relieved there was nothing urgent stopping her aching muscles from reaching her shower and bed.

She woke up a bit past noon, not exactly revived, but resigned to dealing with more clean-up. Her workshop, long-standing sturdy barn that it was, was in great shape, and she'd deliberately set her home on a high foundation, since she'd also set it in a bit of a hollow. After a few hours of clearing debris from sodden flowerbeds and tangled paths, she gave in and texted Dante.

It wasn't, at all, because she was trying to take care of him.

> Amalia: How's the day going?

Dante saw the text as he returned to his van for the clamps Johnny claimed he couldn't find in the exact drawer where Dante kept them.

Hard to fathom it was still the same day he'd woken to after a snooze in her truck, and three scant hours in his own bed, and forty-seven different urgent jobs. Turned out, only a couple dozen were truly urgent, but that was more than enough to send him and Johnny criss-crossing the county all day.

He sat on the edge of the van and texted back.

> Dante: Under control. All ok there?

> Amalia: Ugh. But yeah, only a giant mess.

> Dante: Your climate victory garden survived?

> Amalia: More of the mess, but I think it'll recover. How tiring has your day been?

> Dante: Ugh.

> Amalia: I bet

> Amalia: You going to wrap up any time tonight?

> Dante: In theory

> Amalia: come by if you want. I've got pozole in the crock pot.

Dante blew out a breath he'd held too long. She'd named exactly what he craved. A warm meal, easy to consume, comforting. And Amalia. He craved Amalia, and now she was reaching out to him like she'd seen through his attempts to dam up his feelings and maybe didn't mind them spilling all over her.

> Amalia: not if you're too out of it, of course

> Dante: I am going to get through the rest of the afternoon in better spirits thanks to you. I'll text when I'm on the way.

"You find it, boss?" Johnny ducked his head into the van.

"Yep."

"And they were where?"

Dante tapped a finger against the correct drawer.

Johnny groaned in defeat. It made him laugh, like always, and resolve, like always, to remember his patience.

"I swear I looked in—"

"I know." Dante clapped Johnny on the back as they headed back to the yard with the burst pipe. Inflow, fortunately, unlike the first three pipes they'd reset after the flood-induced subsidence. Damn alluvial plain and damn lax construction engineers to start with.

They got the struts in place and water-pressure tested the joints. After he sent Johnny in the truck to snake out some clogs, he took the van over to the town square to assess if anything had happened with the old sewer line.

He got out and crouched by the temporary covers, where brackish water still glugged from the manhole. Not as much as before, though. He noted the rate of flow and did some quick mental math. With manual pumping, if the rain kept holding off, it might be enough to resolve the problem.

He texted the town engineer, checked his messages, and creaked to standing. There wasn't much of anything else he could complete in daylight hours, even if his body was prepared to stay up all night again.

Bill ambled over as he packed up his van. "Well?"

Dante gave him a rundown of the major problems, pausing often enough to let Bill interject with his opinions about everything wrong, and what infrastructure he'd get in place, if it was up to him.

"Anyhow," he said through a yawn, "we're stable enough, for now."

"If only," Bill said.

"Why? What else happened?"

Turned out two of Honey Wine's three main bridges had sustained damage. The engineers weren't yet saying what repairs would entail. The South Ridge bridge was likely fine except the railings, but the Apple Mill Road one might need substantial work.

"Keep me posted," Dante said, and finally—finally—headed home to clean up. Between the shower, the fresh clothes, and the prospect of spending some low-pressure time with Amalia, he was smiling as he drove to her place.

Amalia's house was softly lit, a beacon in the evening haze. She met him at the door, bright like she hadn't just spent her own day mired in debris. He stepped in and let out a sigh at the smell of simmering pozole.

Amalia took in his damp, neatly combed hair. "Look at you, almost entirely dry."

"I know, right?" He followed the scents deeper into her house.

"Hungry?"

"I think so." Dante rolled his shoulders. "I'm mostly working to convince myself the worst is over, and it's okay to not be on call for a while."

She gave him a clinical head-to-toe look. He was exhausted, and he pretty much longed for her, and that's likely what tempted him to think her look could be a bit admiring, too. "Come on," she said, nudging him into her living room. "Help me shift this."

Together they moved the coffee table to the wall, leaving a

free space across her overlapping rugs. Amalia handed him a yoga mat and unrolled one of her own, and without too much discussion they both moved into sun salutations, followed by a series of slow twists and stretches from the floor. He mirrored Amalia's move into Savasana, and for the first time since before he picked Natasha up for their mess of a date, Dante fully let his stress slide away.

CHAPTER 15

He took over prepping the toppings while she set the table with bowls and drinks. As always, it was annoyingly easy to have him working alongside her in the kitchen. Almost like he could make hanging out easier on her instead of more arduous. Like she'd gone and invited him over both to check in with him, and because her own evening would be better if he was with her.

Which was a ridiculous thought she sent into the ether. Probably she just made too much soup and her freezer was too full for more leftovers.

"Damn, I was so swamped. I forgot to message Natasha. Give me a sec."

Amalia paused in the midst of finding the ladle. "Sure."

She'd gone and banished thoughts of Natasha to the distant past. Which made sense, given how busy they'd been since the previous night. What didn't make sense was the niggling hint of triumph that she and Dante had been messaging all afternoon, but he'd neglected to contact his date. Another ridiculous thought; good thing the ether, unlike her freezer, had plenty of room.

They settled at the table, sharing the various bits of flood-related news they'd accumulated across the day. He insisted on cleaning up, leaving her comfortable and dozy on the sofa while he packed away the leftovers.

The kitchen noises quieted, and she opened her eyes to find Dante propped at the threshold of the living room. He started to say some kind of something, only for his words to get caught by a yawn. He unfurled his arms in an overhead stretch that filled the doorway. "Sorry. I best to head out. Thanks again—"

"No, hang on. You're wiped."

"Yeah." Dante started shaking his head. "That's why."

She was brusque about interrupting him. "Lay down for an hour or two. Hell, sleep over if you want. We've worked too hard to make it through the flooding for you to go and ruin it by running yourself off the road."

After a hesitation that might be as much to do with a foggy, exhausted brain as with his uncertainty, his head dropped into a heavy nod. "Twenty minutes, then I'll be fine."

"Dante, don't be silly. Just stay here tonight." She could follow him home again, if she was so worried. Or drive him back herself. Her logical side offered plenty of solutions besides a sleepover, but the rest of her wasn't listening. It was overwhelmed by the urge to keep him safe under her roof.

He approached the sofa, but she stood and took him by the wrist, leading him down the hall. "You won't fit on my couch. Come on."

At her bedroom door, he halted. "Is this your room?"

She checked his face, but he seemed serious. "Obviously. This is my house, remember?"

"Yeah, but." He fought back another yawn. "You don't have a guest room?"

"I do, but that's where we stuck the home hospital bed when Abuelita got back her mobility." She backtracked to open the door and show him. The mattress was bare, and she'd been using the surface to organize her yarns. "So you'll share my bed. It's big, and it's comfy."

He stopped arguing, maybe because he was asleep on his feet. She found him a spare toothbrush and left him to it, retreating to the living room. Settling into her corner of the sofa, she picked up the anthology she'd been working through. Every time her thoughts drifted towards Dante, dozing in her room, she went back a couple of sentences to refocus on the narrative. It took a buzzingly long time, but she managed to finish the story before succumbing to the temptation of shutting down the house and following him to bed.

She slowed at seeing his dark silhouette against her headboard. There was something absurdly intimate about it, an awareness of him in her space that dragged at her steps as she headed to wash up. But only for a moment.

Changing into sleep shorts, she decided it was because when she'd welcomed men to her bed in the past, they'd hit the sheets together. The new oddness was only because Dante was already sleeping when she came in. She crawled in beside him. Hunched the bedding to her shoulders, as close to the way she liked as possible, given how his bulk disturbed things.

Dante rolled towards her, still asleep. She adjusted the blanket again.

She slept soundly, waking only enough to shift towards Dante's warmth when rain began to tap on the roof. When morning light hit her windows, she came awake fully aware of how comfortably they'd shared her bed. He'd caught hold of her hair, and her fingers brushed his t-shirt. Their feet and legs were a cozy jumble. Dante was motionless, face serene and unguarded. She allowed herself to match his stillness, neither pulling away nor leaning into him. Balanced in a quiet, curious tension about whatever would come next.

If her mom and aunt saw her now, they'd break into their identical grins and start fussing over Dante. They'd snipe at her for not having thrown his clothes in the washer the night before, so he'd have something fresh to wear when he got up. They'd tease her about how he'd have to sit down in all the family photos so he wouldn't throw off the aesthetic balance with his height. They'd press proud kisses to her cheek.

And the galling thing was, she wasn't convinced she would mind.

She wouldn't be doing his laundry ever, but Dante wasn't looking for someone to take over his housekeeping. His vision of settling down didn't seem to include taking anything away from his partner, not her time and not her interests and not her accomplishments. No, what he wanted was to be in service of someone he could celebrate. Just, without having subjected her to the self-improvement he'd recruited Amalia for in the first place. So. That was the established plan, the end.

The first sign of his stirring was that half-smile thing he did, then a lifted chin and a hum, and then, a moment later, the slowest of bleary blinks.

"Well, hi." His morning-rough voice was so much less of a croak than when she'd found him crashed out in her truck. It wasn't smooth like the honey drawl of his daytimes, but whatever vigilant part of her was committed to tracking his rest was pleased. Now if only it would agree to go away and let her live her life unconcerned with whether or not Dante Morales's head spent enough time on his pillow. Or her pillow.

Anyone's pillow. It didn't matter whose, because caring about his sleep was not her task.

Her own voice was a little whispery. "Sleep okay?" And to dispel any ideas he might have about her opting to do anything about it if he hadn't, she added, "You're a cover hog."

"That's why you snuggled up to me, huh?"

Amalia scoffed, but she felt her eyes crinkle in a smile. "If that's what you learned from me correctly pointing out that you're a selfish sleeper, I retract every time I called you a star student."

When she pulled herself away from the warmth of their cuddle, he took over the space she'd left. She didn't dignify his smug stretch, just wrapped herself in her silky shawl and headed to the kitchen.

※※※♥※※※

He burrowed into bedsheets that had captured—lucky bedsheets—sensual impressions of Amalia. Let himself savor the pleasures of the night. The rare depth of his sleep, half-broken whenever she slid towards him. The way he relaxed further into the mattress each time she stole into his space. How the early light streaked towards the dark waves of her hair like it was eager to get caught up in the strands.

It was a bunch of secret knowledge he wasn't likely to get to explore again, so he catalogued it and stashed it deep inside. He'd call it to mind during the times he was mad at whatever fates saw fit to tempt him with a woman too talented and brilliant for his everyday life. Because at least the fates also graced him with one sweet night at her side.

He made his way to the kitchen, eager for coffee. And to hang out with Amalia, to be a friend. "How're the plans for your granny's party?"

She shrugged. "Nothing too new, except Adrian was convinced by the storm that I'm right about renting one of those big canopies for the yard. And my cousins are making a video compilation, so I have to send them my part of that next week so they have time to put it together."

"Warn them to do subtitles. Big ones. We played a video at my aunt and uncle's thirtieth anniversary, and none of the old folks could hear over the chit-chat. Their kids were bummed to have lost points for a sentimental moment."

"This would be your cousins who think roasting you is great sport?"

"Everything's one-upmanship for them. Leo thinks of the video idea and Enrique downloads fancy software to call dibs on making it. Enrique hijacks my dad's ATV to cart inner tubes over to the river, and Leo starts charging people a buck a pop to ride the tubes while he tows them with the ATV."

"I hadn't heard that one."

"There are too many tales for anyone to hear them all, not even the gossipiest gossips in Honey Wine."

She snickered and offered him some of the peanut butter toast she'd made. He sliced an apple to split between their plates.

"Was telling stories about your dating life another contest for them?"

He sank his wince into his coffee cup. Sipped. "Basically. Once Leo heard the report from Jules, they both started seeking out Shawna and other people I'd dated, or anyone those women might have confided in. They might've kept the teasing just in the family, but my primos are not so great at keeping their voices down, or at noticing when there might be others around to overhear."

"Well. Hopefully they'll seek out all the good reports from Natasha and whoever else. I'm sure you'd be able to get Bill and Jackson to spread around that there's more to learn, once you're confident in yourself."

Dante rubbed his forehead. "Doubt Natasha will help there. We hardly spent an hour together before the storm hit."

"Y'all decided not to see each other again? The fact she wanted a good-night kiss didn't change your mind?"

He didn't want to know if that note in her voice was aggravation or hope or exasperation or what. Didn't want evidence of how ready she was to be done with his lessons. Still, she'd told him to bring honesty to their bargain. "Nope. I told you, even if you were right about that, I didn't want to kiss her."

He'd been clear with Natasha, when they'd exchanged messages the night before. For her part, she'd been casual and accepting. That door was closed, even if it might have been wise to leave the idea of Natasha open between him and Amalia. A cushion of deniability, in case his growing feelings about Amalia got to be too fucking obvious for her to ignore.

A call broke his temptation to backtrack. It was Bill Moll, who as always, seemed to have spent all the hours since last they talked networking together every scrap of info he could. He launched into a real detailed account of what was happening with the bridges. By the time Dante returned to help clear the dishes, an idea was bubbling up like groundwater in a spring.

"Listen."

She returned the carafe to her coffeemaker. "Listening."

He scratched the back of his neck. "The bridges are going to be a long-term problem. They'll get them usable for now, but that means industrial patches and temp repairs to the railings."

Amalia grimaced. "Those things suck. Welcome to Honey Wine; please ignore how your view of the bald cypress knees along the Blanco is blocked by prefab steel beams."

"I know, but, listen. What if you covered them up with art installations? Mr. Connor is practically in the palm of your hand now, from what I heard yesterday from everyone talking about how FoundersFest will be better and more inclusive than ever. And if he likes the idea, he'd get the City Council on board. You could do pieces that suit Honey Wine, and your style, and our heritage, and everything we've been saying? And it'll be bright and bold and make the bridges attractive until the permanent repairs are done."

Her eyes widened briefly. "Okay. Wait: yes. Dante! It could be, like, a series of panels. I'll install them right over the ugly."

She moved to the coffee table, started to sit, paced the room again, gesticulating like she was drawing in the air.

Dante followed her; sat in his favorite green armchair. Listened to her ideas blossom.

"I've been planning a series of smaller pieces for the Art Walk, small enough to properly sell out of a booth, but all along they've been—oh, extracts, maybe. Pieces of a whole, in a way. But if I had a canvas like the bridge. Something on display for the whole town, for locals and tourists alike …"

"Visible coming to and going from town. Big enough to be seen as a whole from a vehicle."

"With more detail on the opposite sides, overlooking the water. Good for all the selfies from people walking the banks." She sat, at last, at the coffee table, pulling a notebook and tray of pens out of a drawer. "I can mount them to be moved and redisplayed, maybe as a whole, maybe in sections, depending on who wants to buy them."

"Maybe as a traveling exhibition when the curators come calling."

"Well, that's a dream." Her voice went wry, but he meant it.

"You should dream. You'll show Mike Moll—show everyone—what you've been saying all along about heritage, about your vision, and how it uplifts everyone."

Amalia laughed, and it was so much better than the other times he'd made her laugh. This time, her glee was because she was seeing possibilities he'd help her create. "I love all this. You really think I can get permission for the installation?"

"I think Mr. Connor knows you walk on water. And I bet we could get an article in the paper, and stuff out on socials, to raise money to pay for the art."

She kept sketching. "I'll seek him out in a couple of days, let him see to more urgent stuff first. But any chance you can find me rough specs on the damaged bridges? And info on repair plans, the styles they'll use?"

"Course."

He didn't mean to sound a bit shaky with that last word, but his damn emotions were wreaking havoc inside him. Amalia's excitement shone from her, and if he could take credit for any little part of that, that was a gift. He needed to leave. Meet Johnny and get grounded by whatever nonsense the guy came up with as they tackled the rest of the priority list.

As he pulled on his boots, Amalia came to the door. "Seriously, Dante. Your idea is perfect. If I can pull it off, I'll have something solid to point to with the FoundersFest committee, and a chance to do something ... something that means a lot to me. So thanks."

All he could do was accept her hug, and lock it away with everything else, and go.

CHAPTER 16

She wasn't avoiding anything. Or anyone.

It just happened that between flood cleanup, and wrapping up a commission, and developing a proposal for the bridge art, she was short on spare time. No time she wanted to waste on tolerating her brother's nonsense. No time she'd allow herself to meet the gang at Bob's Bar. And no time, no space in her head, no shred of willingness to develop fucking lesson plans for Dante's plans to fuck anyone else.

And when Livia came strutting through the rolled up door of her workshop, she didn't have anything to feel guilty about. If Livia had time to go bringing containers of the scrumptious muffins she made for her B&B guests to Amalia, she wasn't going to take it in any kind of reproof. Not even when Livia said she was out doing her own reconnaissance on how everyone had fared in the week since the flood.

Livia pulled over one Amalia's rolling stools. "Guess what Jackson told Ellie?"

"Sweet nothings?"

"Ha. Can you picture his pillow talk? It would be recounting every strange truck that pulled into the dump, and what they were tossing."

"You don't know how true that is. Jackson calls me with that kind of news all the time. Do you think Ellie would be jealous?" Jackson Apel ran the county dump and made a point of alerting Amalia when they took in items she could incorporate in her art. She'd eventually set up a dropbox specially for his pictures, since otherwise it got hard to sort through everything he wanted her to browse. And still he'd initially taken Bill's side about her proposal, not because he seemed opposed to change, but because Bill took Mike's side without bothering to hear her out.

"Probably. But yeah, that's not the intel. You'll like this."

Amalia set aside her wheel cutter and checked the sizing of the blue glass she was fitting behind the plasma-cut steel. "Oh?"

"Yep. Jackson was going on about how his forefathers have been in Honey Wine for generations and they've rarely seen a flood like this, blah blah, like climate change is news to him, but then he said how his great-whoever was the one to set up a roller mill up past where RR12 crosses Clay. I will spare you the details of how he convinced everyone that millstones were a thing of the past and roller mills were the wave of the future."

"You're a good friend."

"I know, right? Can I record you saying that for Maggie? I'm trying to bribe her back for another visit and maybe jealousy will goad her into hitting the road."

Amalia opened her arms in invitation, happy to be a prop to return Livia's bestie to Honey Wine. A group of them had had a goofy, giggly sleepover of a visit in the top floor suite of Chata B&B, the last time Maggie had driven down from Dallas, and—whenever she had time for things like fun again—she welcomed a repeat.

After they'd sent a cajoling video message to Maggie, Livia went on to explain how Jackson's relative got in trouble for damming the Blanco too high for his millpond, messing up the town's water source, and how the 1921 floods took out the damn and mill both, and that's when the bridge went up there.

"Hang on, is Apple Mill Road really supposed to be Apel Mill?"

"Probably, but there were some apple orchards along there, too, where it's all pear and peach now. Jackson will tell you every single thing about it if you ask. But, point is, Jackson dug through his scanned archives, and one of the things he found were the old blueprints and sketches for the bridge. And it turns out a man named Andres Hidalgo led the crew building the structure."

Amalia kicked back, a reflexive action that sent her own stool rolling back a couple of feet. "You're shitting me."

"I am not."

"Andres Hidalgo? You're sure? He's sure?"

"He said he'd print out the payroll page and sketches where Andres and Jackson's grandfather made notes. Was he right? Andres Hidalgo was your relative?"

She tapped her sternum, aiming to be calm as she reviewed her history. To not make a mistake. It had to be right, though. "Andres was the father of Abuelita's husband. My great-grandfather. Livia!"

"I know! Told you you'd like this gossip."

"It's not gossip, it's history. This ... when I tell Mr. Connor this? That my installations won't be only aesthetic, won't just charm the tourists."

"Hey, don't knock charmed tourists. I make my living off of charmed tourists."

"I know, and Honey Wine loves them; that's important. But this is more proof of the significance of my heritage here, of how our stories are interwoven with those of the Bohemians. And that's what I'm going to make sure all of Honey Wine understands."

While she waited until after her granny's siesta time, she

pulled up her City Council presentation and added in the documents Jackson had uploaded for her. Andres Hidalgo's signature on the payroll chart, his handwriting on the calculations of piers and notes on who would do the required grubbing—grubbing!—and info Andres wanted sent the state highway department in response to conversations he'd had with the bridge engineer. She'd crossed that bridge innumerable times, and never suspected her great-grandfather had been the head workman in charge of shaping the embankments.

She could use one of Dante's clean handkerchiefs to wipe the leaking emotion off her face.

Abuelita updated her on everyone's storm experiences, as if she hadn't heard them directly already, then asked again for Amalia's account of the night spent sandbagging. It was the most dramatic of the family's rain stories, so her granny was mining her for details to pull out when regaling others.

"So those bridges, the South Ridge and the Apple Mill, I'm making a bid to install art on them while they're waiting on the repairs."

"Beautiful, mija, we can't wait to see them."

"Gracias, Abuela. I hope they let me. And I think you can help. Did you know Abuelo's father at all?"

"Andres, si, por supuesto."

"He lived around here, too? What did he do for his work?"

"How do you think your grandfather learned all that welding he taught you? His father was in construction."

And what would Mike Moll do when she presented her evidence that the Hildagos had worked side-by-side with the Apels and Svobodas, going back to the 1800s? And her family wasn't the only one, of course. Dante had shown her a family tree—not an actual mulberry tree like his surname meant, but a genealogical chart—listing Morales forbearers from when the Hill Country was ruled by the Mexican flag. As with her family, wars and disputes sent them elsewhere at times, but they kept returning to Honey Wine.

She was so busy imagining the beautiful success of their plan—and of putting Mike in his place—that she didn't catch the slip-up that was mentioning Dante to her granny.

Her Abuelita caught it, though. "Dante Morales, eh?"

"The bridge art was his idea." She said it like she was defending him, instead of saying something else entirely to protect herself. Something to convince her granny that there was nothing to read into, no stories to pass around. Shame Dante also managed to be interwoven with all of her flood tales, since it gave everyone twos and twos to incorrectly add up.

At least she'd managed to not mention the night he was too tired to go home. All the time she'd spent pretending to be too busy to hang out with him was paying off.

"You'll bring that nice man to my party, no?"

"I don't know if he's free."

Wrong answer, Amalia. She should've refused. Not allowed the possibility to hang out there, waving a bright flag for her granny's attention.

"You're bringing him. He's been working so hard, helping the whole town since the storms. Plumbers are such steady, reliable people, he deserves the chance to have some fun."

"I'm sure he can manage whatever fun he wants on his own."

"I'm sure he'll have more fun if you take the trouble to invite him to my party. I'm a hoot; he would love to celebrate me."

Probably no one in Elena Hidalgo's long life had managed to refuse her. "I'll see if he can come," Amalia sighed with all the drama of her fiercer younger years. And if that emotions part of her was a little pleased at her granny's insistence, that didn't mean she missed him as anything more than a friend.

It didn't mean she was lying to herself about her stance against relationships, maybe, a little bit, changing.

"No question, he'll be there."

Taking that as a win, Abuelita steered the conversation back to Andres's history and how Amalia could use that to ensure her generation's imprint on Honey Wine was properly recognized. Highlighting the combined European and Mexican influences in a structure as unmissable and symbolic as a bridge would normally be too screamingly blatant for Amalia, but being measured hadn't gotten her close enough to her goals.

So she'd be blatant.

CHAPTER 17

He'd filled up his red notebook in the days since waking in Amalia's bed. Some pages with worksheet answers from the book. Some with stuff he wanted to remember or wanted to explore. Lots of pages with free-wheeling ramblings about ideas that weren't quite from the book, and weren't quite from Amalia, but which were sitting in his way while he thought their questions through.

His macho, showing-off, needing validation problem. That was a grim part to wrestle with. Back when he was with Elizabeth, or anyone, what had he gotten out of it? Setting aside the aftermath and whatever went into the gossip, he'd thought he and Elizabeth had a normal, nice kind of life together. They were both used to their large, close-knit families. They were both spending their mid-twenties focused on building their careers, him through the plumbing ranks and her getting her nursing degree. They had nights out with friends, and he loved her cat, and she often told him he was her hero for doing whatever small household jobs her mother needed.

He told her she was his queen. He told everyone she was his queen. Enrique asked if that meant he was a king or a court jester, and Elizabeth said no, he was her prince. And then Leo made up a jaunty song about a queen kissing her son the prince, and every person at the cookout laughed.

He'd smiled along with Elizabeth's laugh, like the teasing was no bother. But for his bratty little cousins to poke at his happiness, to turn the relationship he was proud of into a joke? He shouldn't have let them realize he could be riled by what they thought. It had provoked them into making sport of him throughout his twenties.

Their nonsense wasn't the real problem. The real problem was why he'd let anyone else's opinion on him and his girlfriend matter so much to him.

Had he been proud of having someone he could label his queen, instead of specifically proud of Elizabeth? She'd been good on her own. Funny. Kind. Driven. And he'd puffed up at having her in his corner. Peacocking around like his pretty partner, someone desirable in looks and in spirit, shone a glorious reflection on himself.

Probably that explained why, when he thought of the breakup, he remembered the joking song, and the way his friend Lee said, "Looks like your pride got curb-stomped in an epic battle." The way he couldn't socialize for months without feeling a virtual spotlight on the empty space beside him, proclaiming to everyone that he was unloved.

He couldn't—wouldn't—let himself get away with that kind of immature, unexamined shit anymore. He needed to learn enough to at least recognize when he should know better.

Should *do* better.

So Dante's goal was to tie his pride up in being a man who listened to his partner. Who held their value separate from his own, a treasure he didn't store in his own trophy case. Who understood he might get side-swiped by ingrained shit, but it didn't have to stop him from moving past all that.

A knock startled him from all the damn introspection. Amalia had invited herself over, and he moved fast to let her in out of the gentle rain. Sliding the red notebook onto a shelf, he offered her a handkerchief and a spot to stow her umbrella.

She wiped drops from her wrists and arms. "You always come through with the clean cloths."

Remembering when she'd called his hankie an accelerator of her libido, he blushed bright enough to spy his red cheeks in the window glass. "Anytime. What can I get you? I'll put on a pot of coffee."

"No, don't bother. A soda would be great, though."

"So, Andres Hildago," he said, settling them in the front room with their drinks. "That's a find."

"Who told you? Greg?"

"You know the Honey Wine grapevine better than that. Greg saying it'd be too direct. That kid who works at the hardware store on weekends, Zeke?"

"Zane."

"Zane, right. We had a call to an antique shop, and Zane's sister works there. She told me."

She laughed. He covered the shiver down his spine by passing over the throw pillow from his side of the sofa.

"Thanks. This town kills me."

"Well, you're gonna slay this town with your installations."

Amalia tossed the pillow back at him. "That was bad. And you're acting like I already got permission and funding."

He crossed his fingers. "You will. Your ancestors are watching to be sure."

She bit her lip. "We'll see. And even if I do, I still have to get Mike to let me into the Art Walk. Realistically, I might end up with only one of those. Or neither."

"Whatever I can do to help, ask." He'd be at Thursday's FoundersFest meeting, of course, but he was at her disposal for anything.

At that, she took back the throw pillow so she could throw

it at him again. "You already helped a ton. I won't let that stop me from asking you for more, but you're the one who broke through Mike Moll's resistance to start with, and the bridge panels? Fucking inspired."

Dante buzzed at her approval. He was so screwed. He should tell her he considered their deal over now.

She spoke first. "Hey, I have two things to ask you now, matter of fact."

He commanded his gaze to move off of how she was tucking herself into a cross-legged position, bolstered by a nest of his pillows. "Yeah?"

"No, it's really three. Or two asks, and a suggestion."

"Done." He held out a hand like he expected her to shake on it.

"Dante. You ever think about how you have no sense of self-preservation?"

Only around her. Not that he was admitting it.

"Fine." He winged his arms behind his head. "Let's hear your demands."

She rolled her eyes. "Okay, so I got the FabConKan gig."

"Fuck, yeah, you did." He held out a fist for her to bump.

"I know, I'm amazing. They're lucky I applied. So ask one is for you to figure out if you're serious about coming with me."

"Easy. Yes." He'd signed up for registration alerts before the flooding. Noted it on his calendar so he wouldn't double-book those days.

"Cool. The other ask is sooner. Will you come to my granny's party weekend after next? She's eager to spend more time with you, which is code for you being interrogated. And if you think she and Adrian are the worst in the family about butting in, you'll learn you're wrong real fast. You'll remember after about three minutes there why you started being so wary about speaking to people in the first place. And since the whole fam will believe you're my boyfriend, only one in five questions—if you're lucky—will be appropriate from someone you just met."

She was flat-out babbling. He'd never thought to witness anything like it.

"Good thing I've never cared what people think of me." *Ha.*

Her eyebrows lifted. "Uh-huh."

"So they'll think things," he said, catching the pillow as she threw it a third time. "What else is new?"

He thought for sure she'd tease him back, but instead she regarded her bare legs like she'd not had enough opportunities to appreciate the supple strength they used to carry her through her life. Or maybe that was just him. He broke into her attention by handing back the pillow.

She said, "As long as you're aware of the gossip this could ignite. It's not like our families keep separate circles. You don't need to decide now. I'll text you the details. You can show up, or not."

Right. He'd not answered her request. "I'm going. Your granny is my favorite."

"Sure, cause you've only met her the once."

"Nah. Cause she's your favorite, too."

She held his gaze, expression gentling to a soft smile. "I'll text it to you."

And suddenly she was decisive, setting her glass on a coaster, striding the few steps to his entryway, making a face at her damp shoes.

But Dante could count, so he moved close enough she'd have to nudge past him to leave. "Amalia."

She squinted up at him like he was something she had to shield against. "Yep?"

He tipped his chin down, closing just a bit more of the distance between them. "What's the third thing I might have agreed to?"

CHAPTER 18

She'd set a trap for herself. Fool. "It's nothing. I've got to get back to the workshop. See you at City Hall?"

"You came over here to ask me two questions you could have texted about."

Where he got off making challenging declarations when her actions were none of his business, she didn't know. "It was on my way."

His half-slow, half-cocked smile tempted her closer. Fool, fool, fool. Every idea she'd ever had was the idea of a fool, and now Dante was seeing the truth of her in action.

"And to make a suggestion. Which you haven't made. Now's your chance, Amalia."

She stepped back like it would help her keep her balance. "I'll text it to you."

"Ha. No you won't." He did the propping himself against a wall thing. Did he think that made him less over-tall? He was wrong.

"It's my choice to suggest or not suggest."

Dante tilted his head. "I know."

"And I don't choose."

He didn't speak, which meant he was waiting for something other than a push out of the way. Maybe he'd say no.

Maybe he'd turn her down. She wouldn't know if she never said it.

She pressed her lips together. "I thought ..."

His attention stayed on her, focused and expectant.

She glanced aside, eyes lighting on his spiral notebook of sex ideas. It was so much more well-used than when he'd first shown it to her. What else would be in his lists? What thoughts had he set out in that careful handwriting of his? What lessons mattered most to him?

She nodded once and mustered her damn voice. "You've got me closer to FoundersFest than I hoped. And beyond that, with the party and the bridges. I think it's time to balance our books some."

Now he was upright, arms crossed and brows low, the very epitome of defensiveness. "What does that mean?"

"You got good at kissing, but we never tested further intimacy. Put theory into practice. And I owe you."

"You ... owe me." Turned out he could cross his arms even tighter.

It was like he wasn't hearing the words she was saying. Like the time she'd spent practicing them to herself, making sure her points were clear, her arguments were sound, was a total waste. Because he was looking at her like she wasn't being honest with him. Or with herself. Or both. "Not that we have scales. But that's my suggestion. More intimacy."

More silence.

So she laid it out. "Sex, Dante. I'm suggesting we find out if you're ready to learn to please your partner in bed."

His body didn't move a single bit for such a long time, but his stance, his attention, his vibe—it was like he'd recoiled from her. Or like she'd shoved him away.

And then, "Oh." He rubbed the back of his head.

"Or not. Like I said, it was a suggestion, not an ask." She twisted, reaching for the door handle.

"Amalia." He was in her space, not quite touching, but close enough. And tense as hell.

"You're the one whose idea it was to get good at sex." She glanced at him, but he was looking at her hands: one holding her umbrella, the other on the door. She set the umbrella leaning against the wall. "You're the one who said I could set the boundaries."

"And now you're changing the boundary so we can fuck?"

Something—the short way he bit out the word, the fact he'd said 'fuck' at all in this conversation—sent her chin up to lock her gaze with his. "You said I make the rules."

"You're talking like I've been keeping a scorecard and now you have to put out. Hell, Amalia, I *know* you don't think that. You'd punch me in the gut if I said that about you. About anyone."

Damn him and his learning how to express his thoughtful nature. She reached out and squeezed his hand. "I'd knee you in the balls, probably. You're right. The balancing books thing, it's not fair. I shouldn't have said it."

She shouldn't have brought the idea of anyone owing anyone else to the table. It wasn't fair to make him hear it, and really not fair that he called her on it. Now she had to do some self-examination about why she'd picked that as the way to proposition him in the first place.

Ugh.

Her eyes were closed, so it was the sound of Dante walking away, and the loss of that interpersonal electricity at her side, that hit her. Part of her longed to hurl herself out the door. All kinds of other places she could be: in her workshop, getting a meal, driving to Austin to spend the night listening to live music. Embarking on a three-week cruise to view some of the world's glaciers before they shrank out of existence.

The rest of her knew better, so she shifted to look, and

found Dante back on his sofa, bent over with his head in his hands.

Ugh, again. She kicked off her shoes, and before she thought better of it, found herself sitting beside him. Didn't touch him, though she wanted to. "I'll leave if you want."

His back shuddered in some kind of dismissive shrug.

Yeah, she'd taken a chicken's way out with that offer. "To be clear, I don't want to leave. And you're right I could've texted you about Kansas and the party. But I had to ask you, in person, about us having sex. And trust me, despite all your help, that's not the only reason I suggested it."

He muttered something that was muffled by his palms.

Amalia slid closer and leaned a little into his shoulder. "What?" she asked, voice low.

As Dante straightened, his arm ran up along hers. She made no move to change that.

"I asked—how much of it is from obligation? Your offer?" His cheeks had rusty flags of emotion. Stress? Embarrassment? Anger?

She probably was flushed, too. "Despite my ... clumsy words, believe me, I don't feel obligated. That was a shield I put up to spare myself if you weren't interested. Aren't. In case you aren't interested."

His eyes were particularly sad and she couldn't deal with it. "Amalia. Communication and honesty goes both ways."

"I get it. I said it was a mistake." She blew out a gust of air and stood. "It's fine, Dante. I'll see you later."

This time he didn't follow, so she shoved on her damp shoes and decided dashing to the truck was a better plan than pausing to unfurl her umbrella. The raindrops practically sizzled on her hot cheeks, but nothing drowned out Dante calling after her.

"Amalia. Wait, hold up."

He hadn't stopped for his raincoat. He stood there, feet and jeans and shirt getting increasingly soaked, chest moving like the few feet from his door to the sidewalk were some kind of odyssey.

In some kind of half-trance, she opened the umbrella over them both. Never mind that water still dripped out of his hair, or that holding it high enough for him meant she was protecting only a fraction of herself. She said, "Okay."

"Okay?" His tone was as ragged as his breath.

"You said to wait." With her free hand, she wiped her face. Lowered her voice like it would cut through the rainfall better that way. "I'm waiting."

Intent as fuck, he stepped closer to her. Pressed their bodies together, wrapped his arms securely around her waist. His own voice was low, and slow, and wry. "Sorry. I'm getting you wet."

She squinted at the devil twinkles in his eyes. "You're not funny."

He might have been trying to hide his smile, but the quirk of his cheek betrayed him. "Okay."

"Also, in case you forgot, I'm still waiting." Waiting with her arm curled up around his upper back, but he could figure out that part without her having to name it.

They were close enough that the deep breath he drew expanded his chest into her body. "I'm interested. If you're sure it's what you want. If you want it because we—because you desire it … not because of our deal? Because you're as curious about sex with me as I am with you? Then I am, too."

CHAPTER 19

Without warning, her laugh rang out over the rain.

"Is that a yes?" he asked. His heart was doing silly things that set him afire.

"Hell, yes."

He locked their hands together—slippy wet but still somehow electric—and led her to his house. She bumped into his back in the foyer, dropping the umbrella back on the tiles and kicking her shoes towards the wall.

When he turned, he was sure his face gave everything away. So he may as well get verbal about his fears, like the communicator he was aiming to be. "You'll stop me if I suck?"

"I mean. Redirect you, more likely, because I'm in this for my own sake, too, you know." The way her eyes skimmed over his sodden body told him she expected to find what she wanted from him.

He'd been met with those looks before. This time, he wasn't turning into a mannequin. "I don't think a handkerchief is going to be enough this time. Want to grab a shower, or maybe we ought to strip off and see what happens."

She tossed her hair back, then collapsed snickering against

him like she was letting him be the structure she needed to take form. He hugged her, and they were both cold and damp, but it didn't bother him at all.

He dropped a kiss to the top of her head. He'd seen that move in plenty of shows, and never understood it. It looked from the outside like babying the woman, treating her as some little miss that needed protecting. But between him and Amalia, none of that applied. And even with her damp scalp and his increasing awareness that these jeans weren't broken in enough to be worn in the rain, he understood something so new about it. Kissing the top of her head meant he had permission to be affectionate when she wouldn't see it coming. It meant they were already right up against each other, and had plans to keep that going. It meant he wanted her aware of his desire, and it kinda also meant he was letting that clever brain of hers know he admired it.

So he did it again, then showed her the way to his room.

"How big is your shower? And if the answer is only big enough for one of us, I hope you know I'm calling dibs."

He grinned. "I did know that. Did you know I'm a plumber?"

She stopped short, giving him a look like he'd told her the best-ever secret. "Dante Morales. Do you have a fancy bathroom in this pin-neat little house of yours?"

He shelved her opinion of his home for later, and gave as much flourish as he had in him while swinging open the door to his en suite.

Amalia breathed out a low whistle. "Oh, my fucking God." Her socks left squelchy prints on the floor as she spun in the room, taking it all in like his bath fixtures were whichever kind of art she wished there was more of in Honey Wine's galleries.

"I knocked out a couple of closets to make room for the tub." He was tall. No point installing a jetted tub if he couldn't sink into it when he needed it.

"Who needs closets? I had to install drawers in mine. Hanging things up is a waste of space you can use putting in dual shower heads."

"And a tankless hot water heater."

"Damn," she said. "That's sexy." She stripped off her wet shirt and tossed it at him before opening the frosted glass shower door to crank on the water. By the time he'd decided to drop her clothes in the tub, she'd peeled off her leggings and socks and was testing how quickly his heater—literal, this time—got to work.

He leaned against the sink to work down his jeans, cursing himself for wearing them, and blessing the denim at the same time for giving him a focus beyond all the delicious skin Amalia had revealed.

"What do you think?" he asked, once he'd made a loose ball of his pants and shirt and tossed them in his hamper. "Big enough for two?"

She snagged his wrist and dragged him in with her. Didn't wait to see if he'd manage getting out of his boxers before catching his face and pulling him down and capturing his mouth in a kiss.

Once more, his whole world went liquid. All the steam, all the heat, all her bared skin for him to explore. Tension and questions and nerves went swirling down the drain with the deliciously hot water. Her mouth opened to his in one of those demands that wasn't a demand at all—just a reminder of all she'd already taught him—and he curled his hands around her waist in response. Maybe he could be good at this after all.

He lifted her just enough to feel like he'd done something about the height difference between them, just enough rub their skin together and elicit a noise from her throat that suggested he keep it up. Judging by her leg wrapping around his, her hand stroking his back, her hips dancing to his, he might manage to be very good.

"Amalia."

"Dante."

And then they were kissing again. His blood was hotter than the water, scalding him from head to toe, but he remembered to let the desperate wanting move through him without letting all his accelerators take over.

It felt like triumph, when he felt her slow their movements and he took her cue. When he responded to her gentle fingers sweeping his shoulders and arms, by scooping the wild mass of her hair out of her face, and shifting them so he could tilt her head back under the nine-inch spray head and hit the button to switch it from rainfall to a concentrated stream.

"I don't have much in the way of product," he said, pulling bottles of shampoo and 3-in-1 wash off the rack.

"That's okay." She took the body wash and a mesh sponge. "I don't need to wash my hair. Any chance you have a hairdryer, though?"

He dropped a kiss to her shoulder, which was another way he was trying to keep in control and not memorize the sight and taste and touch—God, touch!—of her every inch. "No, but—"

"You're going to say you'll buy one before the next time I come over, aren't you?"

The woman really did have the measure of all of his flaws. "I get the impression that'd be bad."

"See? You're learning."

She'd covered very little of her skin with suds. It was worse than her t-shirt plastered to her in the rain. Worse than being naked and skin-to-skin under the spray. All teasing temptation and the promise of exploring her when she smelled like his.

He dropped a kiss to her other shoulder—this bending to kiss her thing was addicting—and stepped out to get her a fresh bath towel.

⇢»»»♥«««⇠

She was being covetous. And she was rejecting any pesky thoughts that she shouldn't relish all the things she was getting. A gorgeous shower. Increasingly talented kisses. The look in Dante's eyes as she dried herself with fluffy plush terrycloth.

Before she'd made her plans to proposition Dante, she'd taken stock of her goals. Because she was smart, and driven, and wasn't putting some guy ahead of everything else in her life. Not even the guy who'd been helping her with those goals.

So she'd shown up ready for anything. Well, not ready to express her desires in quite the right way, but they'd dealt with that. And now they were clean, and dry, and right next to his neatly made bed.

It almost was cute, how tidy he kept his home. Not because it was the opposite of how her family would expect a man's lair to look if he lived on his own—though they absolutely would be surprised by Dante's neatness. No, it was the precision and balance everywhere. Matching lamps on the matching side tables bracketing a bed with a blanket folded into tidy thirds at the foot and matching pillow shams at the head.

And the two of them, wrapped in matching towels.

Of course she followed her urge to mess up his sense of order. It was her mission, wasn't it, to break him out of his old patterns? She'd certainly gone and broken out of her own, showing up at the house of this ultimate relationship guy, and propositioning him.

She dropped her spent towel on his floor and came up behind him, winding her arms around his waist and pressing up against his back, plastering herself there and propelling them both onto the mattress.

He made a strangled noise as he tumbled. Amalia

stretched out beside him with nothing but the knot of his towel between them. It didn't stay that way long. "Can I?" she asked, dancing her fingers over it. At his desperate nod, she tugged it loose and let her hand fall, firm and intent, on his hip.

"Think you can be as good in bed as you were in the shower?"

"Yeah." He swallowed. "I hope, yeah."

"Cause I think it's time we fuck. If you agree."

"I'm offering you my enthusiastic consent."

"Damn." She licked her lips. "That really is sexy. I mean, it doesn't hurt to hear it said by a hot, naked plumber."

He stopped staring at her breasts long enough to check out her smile. "Are you mentioning my job so you can start in with the laying pipe jokes again?"

"Only if your enthusiastic consent is for that, too."

He laughed, and when he laughed, he un-froze. With a hand on her back, he encouraged her to meet his kiss. He rolled to face her and finally, at last, like touching her was a prize he didn't want taken away, dragged the backs of his fingers across her nipples.

The noise she made was ferocious and happy. He pressed closer, his leg hitched over her hip. "Amalia, I like touching you so damn much."

"Hmm. Sounds like a plan. But hey, do you have protection in here, or do I need to go back out to my truck?"

He snorted. "Don't forget the umbrella."

Those eye glints were in full force, and she played along, pushing herself up like she was heading outside. "Did you see where I dropped my keys?"

"Shut up." He pointed his lips over her shoulder. "There's condoms in that nightstand there. They're up to date—I don't risk anyone's reproductive freedom in this state."

"You've already got me wet for you, buddy, you don't need to gild the lily. Speaking of: any lube? Or toys?"

Dante smashed himself into the mattress, groaning. "You don't make it easy for me to keep a foot on the brakes."

That thrill suffused her limbs again. "How about this? How about we take it for granted that you are all about the acceleration, but for now your job is to stay in park. I'll guide you along, and you speak up about what works or doesn't, but unless I'm telling you what to do, you just … stay good and still for me."

CHAPTER 20

Oh fucking hell and all the stars in the sky.

With more effort than it ought to take to speak while laying perfectly still on his own bed, Dante said, "Yup. Yeah, okay. That's good. I agree."

Amalia had his full attention—shit, she had all of him—and he was pretty sure she knew it. Her leg wound over his, and her hand covered his, pulling it to rest on her chest. "You like touching me so damn much," she said. "So how about you keep at it?"

He almost didn't trust himself to move. She was there, right there, for *him*, somehow. And he would not go back to being a mannequin, so, like Amalia asked, he kept touching her.

He explored those firm breasts that cushioned the strength in her chest. Teased and squeezed and watched her. Listened to her. Pieced together the line between too gentle and too firm, and the pleasure she got from tongue and lips and teeth.

The pleasure he gave her.

He learned the catch in her breath, the arch of her spine, and as soon as he thought maybe he was getting it right, she nudged his hand down. Dragged their linked fingers along one thigh and rested his palm on her center.

They both groaned.

Dante forced himself not to thrust his hips against her, or flip them so he could send his hands roaming everywhere, or beg her to sheath his cock.

"Remembering the anatomy diagrams from the book?" Her teasing tone reined him in. Tied his heart tighter to her.

He licked his dry lips. "Labia major and labia minor, and so forth."

She smirked at him. "Go on."

And he did, with his fingers and his words and his focus on every move he helped her make. "Pubic mound, vaginal opening. Those sheltering lips and the lubrication from your glands."

"I think you forgot something. And you can't win the star student award if you don't know it."

"Your powerful thighs? Your gorgeous ass?"

Amalia squeezed those thighs together and clapped her hand over his, so he was trapped in the heaven of her most intimate space. "I want to tell you this is all hitting my brakes, but all that attentive curiosity of yours won't let me get away with the lie."

Dante lent in for a long kiss, then sent his attention to her collarbones, her neck, her belly. Finally he pushed back enough to see, to memorize and relish, that favorite, delicate, sensual place.

"Clitoral hood," he said, low and tight. His thumb traced it in a gentle circle. "Where the magic concentrates. Where you throb and swell and where, if I do things right, you ache for my touch."

Her legs relaxed open. She planted a hand on his hip. Dug in.

"Clitoral legs." He let his fingers run down each side of her labia. "Hiding all those nerves that'll surround me when I'm inside you. Sending sensations deep, encouraging your walls to squeeze so I know we're in it together."

She was rapt on him now, her breath juddering and her hips twitching. It was some kind of miracle, learning these deep secrets of Amalia's body. "More. Find my clit again. Circles and, like, little pinches, but not right on the hood."

And he did, and she flexed her hand in his hair. And he ducked his head to nibble her neck, and groaned, and her body bucked at his. Her nipples stood erect, she moaned his name and juddered and peppered kisses on his ear, his cheek, his nose. His lips.

It was all fucking astounding.

And agonizing, because. She wanted him to be still. And he wanted to move. To claim and thrust and tongue and thrust and celebrate, knowing he'd done it. He'd made this extraordinary woman orgasm.

But he'd agreed to be good for her, so he bit down on his pleas and watched as Amalia's trembles settled down. Moved his hand from her core and dragged up the blanket from the foot of the bed. Smoothed it over her, but, carefully, not over himself. His cock was so hard he worried that the blanket's slight friction could set him off.

Eventually, blissfully, she roused enough to deliver a sharp nip on his shoulder.

"Fuck," he groaned.

"Star student."

"Hmm. Glad to know it." Even he could hear the brat in his voice.

It earned him another nip. And feather-light fingers brushing away any hurt. "Condoms to my right, you say?"

⇥⋙♥⋘⇤

Languorous didn't cover it. Amalia was boneless; all she wanted to do was lay there and thrum with aftershocks and eventually conk out into a sex coma and wake up and set him to work again. Thursday's FoundersFest meeting could go on without her; she'd be busy not leaving Dante's bed.

But if they stopped now, it turned into just a lesson. She didn't owe him sex, but she wanted them both to get to fuck. She shifted, flipping herself to flop over him like a cat wanting someone to put down their book and pay attention. "And that consent is still in place?"

"Can't believe you have to ask." His voice came tight, and his cock twitched against her bare belly. It set her buzzing again, and he saw it in her smile. She sat back enough to snatch a condom from the nightstand. He gripped the sheet by his sides.

She pat his chest to thank him for being so good. Also because his chest was a soft-furred, hard-planed, sweat-warmed wonderland.

Every movement was exertion in her delicious, post-orgasm state. Almost as bad as clearing out her yard after laying flood control all night. She pushed herself upright. Shifted up his body until he was poised at her entrance.

Dante whimpered and bent his legs so she could balance against his thighs. And maybe so he had better range of motion for thrusting.

"Here," Amalia instructed, passing him the condom. Aching as she was to have him inside her—to reward him for being so goddamn good—she could only muster so much control, and touching his cock would blow it.

He rolled it on with unsteady hands. Her legs were open wide now, but he still didn't move. He waited on her own slow slide to take him deep. Letting him know what worked sure wasn't something Amalia needed to verbalize right now; her groan ripped from her throat as soon as his length pressed and stretched into her walls.

As her pelvis met his, Dante caught his breath and flexed his hips and practically melted into the sheets as his diaphragm contracted. It was a groan, a sigh, a strong sharp laugh.

He stilled again, and Amalia bit her bottom lip to stop from absolutely glowing her delight at him. "This hard for you?"

Dante narrowed his eyes. "Shut up."

"Remember when you asked if there was room for two? You got an answer to that yet?"

"Amalia, so help me." He inched a tense hand towards her clit.

"Touch me and I'll recite Cosmo Castorini's 'Three Kinds of Pipe' speech at you."

He whipped his head to the side and threw one of those beefcake arms over his face to cover his snorts. It was perfect; exactly the reason she'd been watching *Moonstruck* clips in the first place. Dante was desperate. On edge. Holding himself back so she could get her jollies before he did.

Distracting him with nonsense made her giggle—hello, happiness as accelerator—and, she suspected, gave him back the measure of control he needed to stay in this nice, slow, hot moment with her.

When he looked at her again, she leaned in for a kiss. Made it leisurely, set up a rhythm of almost kneading his shoulders as she stroked chest to neck to biceps to chest again. He locked his hands on her ass and behaved almost like his pulse wasn't racing. His shallow moaning gasps gave him away. His constantly rocking pelvis. The wide wildness in his eyes.

She'd pushed him as far as she could. She wanted those jollies, all of them, and immediately.

Amalia clamped her core around his cock. "The only pipe I use," she growled.

Smart man, he took her quoting Cosmo as the cue it was, and had her clit between two knuckles in an instant. She grabbed his headboard and his shoulders and anywhere she could get some leverage to ride him hard. She was all gas, no brakes, nodding at him to do the same when her breath was too harsh to give him the words.

His hands roved everywhere, sensations that lit sparks each place he touched. Skin and laughs and each other's names. So much motion, such a vast break from his earlier hard-fought stillness, and then. And then: one firework of a touch sent her up in flames, left her vibrating and grinding into him.

A beat later, a roar like thunder, and his tension broke hard. He arched and thrust and pulsed. He cursed, but it was a blessing. A benediction. Grace.

The best kind of collapse left her breathless and panting and grinning into his chest. She nipped his pec, and he laughed, and she rolled off him onto his mussed-to-hell sheets.

While he dealt with the condom, she recollected his neat-and-tidy instincts and managed to move enough to smooth the fitted sheet snugly in place and pull the top sheet and blanket into order. He smiled at how she'd left a corner tucked back so he could crawl in beside her. He floated the covers atop her sated body and tucked them around her shoulder. It was too damn cozy, and a half-alert part of her brain remembered he'd observed her that way when she'd let him sleep in her bed.

"Star student," she accused, and watched the peace in his smile as he winked, or maybe blinked, and sighed himself to sleep.

CHAPTER 21

He'd tried to wake Amalia when he was roused for an early callout. Shame it was too complex for him to let Johnny work on alone. He couldn't do more than dispatch his apprentice to prep the site while he set out some breakfast options in the kitchen and jotted a note about the coffee maker's quirks.

And then the demands of plumbing took over his day. A usual kind of workload—scheduled jobs and emergencies and a fellow subcontractor who threw everyone else's plans awry and blamed it on one of the most reliable suppliers they knew.

By lunchtime he'd checked his phone a hundred times too many and not gotten a reply to either of the texts he'd left for Amalia. It turned him into a bigger grump than he should be, by any rights. She'd muttered a farewell before burrito-ing herself back to sleep that morning, and hadn't acted like she needed to talk him through anything. Plus they'd see each other at the FoundersFest meeting, and she knew she only had to ask if there were more ways he could help her there.

Johnny was slicing four inch PVC with Dante's Sawzall when Amalia called. He ought to keep trenching for the drainage lines, stay on track for what they planned to grind through by end of day.

Instead he shook off his gloves, jammed his thumb in one ear to block the whir of the blade, and hustled around the corner to hear her better. "Hey."

"Howdy."

"Everything go okay this morning? You got your coffee?"

"Dante." Her tone did that shields-up thing. "Are you fishing for compliments? Because I'm still me, in or out of our original deal. I don't stroke egos."

"Right." He nodded like that could help her believe his words. But, no. Honesty. "Amalia, I don't need you to make up nice things to say, but: I'm still me, too. Believe me, I trust that if I'd messed up—last night, or this morning—you'd say so."

"And I didn't do that."

He found himself bouncing on the balls of his feet, and dropped to a squat to focus his energy. "Nope. You only stroked things that aren't my ego."

She snorted. "Good of you to recognize the difference between your dick and your ego."

He bit his lip to stop from snickering at her. "See, is that difficult? A nice affirmation, now I'm happy, and you didn't have to shower me with praise."

"You're ridiculous is what you are."

"Now I'm blushing."

"Shut up. I only called to tell you my family's going to the FoundersFest meeting, so I'm driving over with them. I'll see you there."

She didn't indulge in niceties before hanging up, but Dante could read into the call if he wanted to. Instead of texting her meeting logistics, she'd called, and that meant she wanted to hear his voice, like he did hers. It wasn't a bouquet of compliments, but the happy implications kept him going strong for the last stretch of his ten-hour day.

Not even Johnny's ribbing about how his mood reversed after he ran off to take a call stopped him from whistling while he finished his work.

※※※♥※※※

City Hall's parking lot was full enough that they dropped Abuelita and Tío Leon at the door, and the meeting room was packed. Not like last time, when she'd walked in knowing she was the burr in everyone's side, and sure it'd be a moment's work for them to flick her ideas to the trash.

When she and her parents walked in, the sea of faces was familiar, and mostly friendly. Her family, her fellow artists— she detoured to thank Jorge's basket-crafting neighbors for attending—people she'd worked alongside during the flood. Some of the ranchers she'd sat with in the wet early hours at the Honey Wine Cafe gave her that chin-jerk greeting so beloved by taciturn Texas men. She gave it right back. Her preconceptions insisted they were more likely to have shown up to align with the old-guard arguments, but then again … None of them had been involved with the festival in the past, and it was obvious most of the new attendees were clustered among her people.

Ellie'd claimed she'd been talking up her bridge proposal and the expansion of the festival. That people had asked how they could champion her—and they'd actually followed through and shown up.

Tía Cecily flagged them down. She'd commandeered a quadrant of seats, and was directing her brother to squeeze in a few more folding chairs, absolutely disrupting the neat rows Mr. Connor would preside over. "Hey, my sweet. Your boyfriend is coming tonight, yes? We should save him a spot?"

Her aunt was provoking her out of love, giving her a little battle to focus on so she wouldn't direct all her nerves to the bridge beautification discussion. It was one of her favorite stage mom tactics, but knowing the score didn't mean it didn't work. Having her nerves understood like that, having this familial show of force—even if they were supporting her while they thought she was bending to their will about relationships—it filled her heart.

"He's sitting with our friends up front. Y él no es mi novio."

Not that Cecily listened to her protest. She'd grabbed hold of Amalia's arm and craned round to look at Dante and them.

She knew exactly where he was, of course. She'd waved as they all entered, and every step since, she'd felt that annoying connection that came from him watching her. Waiting for her to make the first move. Using those soulful eyes to let her know it was up to her to put any kind of claim on him, and his attention to let her know he was willing to be claimed.

Amalia worked to construct the perfect smile to show him. Calibrated her expression to hide—from Dante; from their friends; from herself—any clues about how much she wanted to plant her excitable heart right near his. But also to let him know, she hoped, that she appreciated his seeing and understanding her need to focus on the meeting and her family. There were too many strands coming together at once, and she had to keep her professional, artistic, and community-building goals uppermost.

Cecily rattled instructions at Tío Leon and navigated Amalia across the tide of people until they'd reached her friend group. Amalia tried to effect introductions, but one of the ways Tía Cecily occupied herself, instead of by pursuing her creative interests, was by being one of those knows-every-one-at-first-sight people.

"So you're the heroic plumber who saved the town, then? You have our thanks."

Dante fell for the blatant flattery. "Oh, thank you, but no, señora. I was one of so many, including your lovely niece here."

Out of Cecily's sightline, she rolled her eyes at Dante. He lifted his shoulders in the slowest, shallowest shrug.

One single night of fucking didn't mean his eyes should be glinting at her so much. Even when, thanks to all the eye contact during those rounds of fucking, she could read his non-verbal message just fine. It wasn't in her plan for him to be so blatant.

Her aunt had no issues with blatant, though. She glanced over her shoulder at Amalia's family, then performed an exaggerated double-take. "Mija, oh dear, I didn't realize my neighbor was coming tonight. I need to talk to him. About snap peas. You don't care if he sits with us, do you? You can stay up here with Dante and everyone. Dante, you'll take care of my sweetie?"

And then Tía practically shoved her into the empty chair beside Dante before setting sail for the far side of the meeting room.

※※※♥※※※

He sat facing the podium, arranging himself so no parts of his too-eager body touched any part of her. They were attending a big important meeting where she would either power towards, or get rebuffed from, her big important goals. It was not the right time to prioritize his urge to touch her, even if he hadn't shown up unsure of what she wanted in terms of publicly linking herself to him.

Amalia's ideas on expanding FoundersFest were already an accomplishment—he'd never thought to see so many white Honey Wine citizens rallying around to say that it mattered to them, recognizing the work of non-Europeans in building their town. He was proud if he'd done as much as she claimed to help her get out her message. And now, with

Mr. Connor calling everyone to order, he could tell she was brimming with determination to convert all the good will in the room into concrete action.

But he was hard-pressed not to wrap his arm around her shoulders and shake her in triumph when Mr. Connor stopped Mike Moll from bulldozing his way into speaking out of turn. Instead, he took happiness from the way she elbowed him after Mr. Connor emphasized that they would stick to the published agenda.

Every committee had suggestions for adding Tejano traditions in the mix along with the usual Texian ones. Some were more enthusiastic than others. Bob was geeking out about the lineup for the music stage, when Mike huffed and made his way to the podium.

"I believe I'm allowed to speak now." He gave Frank Connor a look like he thought he'd have to bring his own bullhorn to be heard. Mr. Connor's smile was tight as he adjusted the mic to Mike Moll's height. "Before I get into my report, let me tell y'all about a great idea I had for Apple Mill and South Ridge bridge repairs. Since South especially is a major corridor for visitors to Honey Wine who are touring the Painted Churches, I think we should shield the construction ugliness with scrims decorated in the tradition of our community's Painted Churches. Maybe even blown-up images from inside the churches themselves. And we can add the FoundersFest website to the scrims."

Dante's ears worked fine, so that wasn't the problem. He really was hearing Mike flat out steal his and Amalia's plan. Not even acknowledging all the work she'd put into research and mocking up images, the time she'd taken to calculate what would most enliven the bridges. Not just for tourists, either, and could Mike be more biased towards them as his main source of income? The town lived largely off of a tourism economy, but all those people working to make things appealing to tourists saw the bridges every single day, not just for a picturesque weekend.

He pushed to his feet, ready to speak truths about dismissing the ideas of a brown woman, about caring for every resident Honey Wine, about valuing new art alongside those traditional crafts. But Amalia tapped her foot to his ankle. He shot her a glance that took in her pressed lips, her firmed chin, her brow shielding eyes that were aimed like lasers at Mike Moll.

When she'd told him she needed help with the festival in the first place, she wasn't looking for someone to make her arguments for her. He was the one who'd had to learn to conduct conversations better; she was the one who gave him the talking points. His use to Amalia was only in making people more amenable to listening to what she had to say.

She wouldn't want him flying off the handle on her behalf.

He held the back of her chair as she stood, then put himself back into the audience full of people primed to listen to her.

"Mr. Connor, I've got something to say."

Mike paused like he expected Mr. Connor to stop her for speaking out of turn. But when Mr. Connor gestured for her to continue, Mike lifted his hands in a performative not-my-fault kind of way.

"You mentioned beautification for the bridges while they're under construction. I've been working on ideas for that." She pointedly did not look Mike's way. "Working with the engineering and permits departments, specifically, but also consulting other local artists. Our proposal is for custom work that draws on the traditions of every community that has come together to form Honey Wine. You'll be happy to hear one of the ideas is a modern reimagining of the Painted Church style. Know what that artist told me? That there's a cluster of those churches that had their spire crosses made by a well-known blacksmith.

He was one of the Black Freedmen who settled in Green's Prairie. So let's not ignore that it wasn't just the Czechs who created those famous churches. But the reason this is all relevant to FoundersFest is that the bridge art will be installed throughout the Festival period—City Hall has my detailed timelines on file, and my budget estimates—but also because when we expand the mission of FoundersFest to honor all of our founders, we can feature those local creators as part of the Art Walk."

"The Art Walk is nearly booked up, if you'd let me read my committee report."

Dante wasn't the only one muttering at Mike Moll's obstinance. The crowd in the room palpably glared at him.

"Then it's great news that some of the artists you've booked are already on my roster, isn't it?"

Mike crossed his arms. "I thought you were taking over the bridges just for yourself."

She paused like she was letting that statement sink in for everyone in the meeting room. "Huh. So you did know about my proposal before you countered with yours?"

Mike turned nearly purple at that, and Dante figured Amalia must have fully given up on the idea of her work ever being featured in Moll's on Main. Not that she needed the buy-in of one mean small-town gallery owner. Her vision and her talent were too great to stay stuck in Honey Wine, so Moll's was no loss.

Mr. Connor leaned into the mic. "Amalia Reyes brought us the temporary bridge beautification project, which the Council is very excited about. We are particularly grateful for someone with her experience creating metal installations, since she understands exactly what will go into working with the construction crews and mounting the displays. We were prepared to sign off on using panels entirely created by Amalia, but she asked us to hold off while she consulted other artists. Not everyone is prepared to work on the required large scale, or able to meet the deadlines, but we believe the people she's recruited are going to enhance the experience of FoundersFest for everyone. Which is why we've passed a motion to proceed with her plans. We planned to notify you once we finalized the funding, but since, ahem, it came up today: congratulations, Ms. Reyes."

Amalia's family let out some whoops of approval. She grinned over at them, doing little to suppress her delight at Mr. Connor's announcement. Dante wanted to grab her and spin her in a triumphant circle, but: wrong time, wrong place.

After that, everything moved fast. The committee passed a vote to approve the expansion of FoundersFest's mission. Mike pocketed Amalia's list of suggested Art Walk additions —she'd cleverly printed it out, including links to sites and thumbnail images of their work. Mr. Connor called the meeting over. Amalia's family drew her into chatter and celebration.

And she drifted out, caught up in their wake, without once pausing to spend a private moment with him.

CHAPTER 22

It wasn't as if she didn't want to spend time with him. That wasn't why she'd let her family spirit her away at the end of the meeting—the meeting that had gone even better than she'd dared to hope, the meeting where half the people in attendance were there thanks to Dante's encouragement to give her a chance—and it wasn't why he hadn't heard from her since.

The truth was, she was swamped. A good kind of swamped, but still: swamped.

And also: she was lying to herself, because damn if she had figured out if she wanted more sex with him, or not. Well, no. She knew she wanted more sex. But did she want all that came with it—going on dates, and people talking about them as a unit, and most of all, the constant managing of her family's expectations? It felt like the kind of weighty choice she shouldn't make on a lust-fogged whim.

She'd meant to call him the day after the meeting, but then a call came in from City Hall to say they were prioritizing moving her permits through. Mike Moll had rallied a few folk to his side to complain about his treatment. Well, about some made up shit to do with county and town boundaries and who should qualify to exhibit at FoundersFest, but it was the same thing. So all of Friday she spent re-confirming her specs for the town, and following up with her collaborators. And the weekend went to taking her granny shopping for party supplies, because, after all, she'd told Abuelita she'd happily be on call for errands.

And her career was her priority. Her friends, her family, walks to enjoy wildflower season: all of that mattered, too.

Knotting herself up about Dante's feelings was not a priority.

So she appreciated Dante's texts about how she'd rocked the meeting, and about how Johnny was on quest to discover new curse words he could get away with in front of customers, and with a downright artistic photo of Bill Moll and Jackson Apel laughing about something outside the hardware store. But it wasn't her job to keep telling him he was a good boy.

Like he'd said, he knew she'd let him know if she was unhappy with him. And if she was avoiding him because she had to sort out her feelings, he would know that wasn't a criticism. It was only taking the space she needed to think about what she wanted.

To think, too, about how he'd never asked her for anything more than a night of sex. He hadn't even asked for that—it had been her idea. So if she got somewhat grumpy about not knowing if he'd return her sentiments, that was for her to figure out, too.

She'd promised to invite him to Abuelita's birthday party, though. Before heading to her workshop, Amalia fired off a quick message with details about Saturday. And then she finished up two sculptures, and framed out another, in a burst of productivity so intense her muscles sang. It felt damn good to be busy.

It also felt lonely.

She ignored that and tackled the next items on her priority list.

Three days before the party, they'd still not seen each other, but were back into the habit of semi-regular texting. She offered to pick him up on the way, which forced her to think about how that would mean extra time together, and keeping an eye out that he wasn't bored and restless to leave, and having him by her side as he met everyone he'd not met at the meeting. Most of her family had already decided they were dating, so they could just as well walk in hand in hand, as far as that crowd was concerned. But there were plenty of others who'd be celebrating her granny's birthday, and it was possible that a few of them didn't already think she was besotted with the man.

When she got to his house, she discovered he'd made suppressing her feelings harder by looking so fucking good. It wasn't like she never seen him in his nice jeans and a button-down. He'd been dressed the same for that date with Natasha.

But now that she knew what was under the clothes, all those buttons between her and his deliciously hairy chest were damn distracting.

Also, he did his slow half-smile when he opened the door to her, and no rational person could resist swooning at that.

She cleared her throat. "Hey."

He looked her over, lingering on where the hem of her skirt fluttered around her knees. "Well, hi."

She forced her hands to stop smoothing the fabric. "I can wear skirts. It's not unheard of."

"Not complaining, Amalia. You look beautiful. As always."

She bit her lip and glanced away, because he made it difficult to be rational. "Thanks. You ready?"

He picked up a gift bag and followed her. Once in the passenger seat, he said, "It's real nice to see you again."

Amalia countered with, "You didn't need to bring a gift."

"It's a weighted lap blanket. Not too heavy. I read it'd be good for her arthritis, maybe."

He was killing her with his sweetness. Instead of dealing with that, she told him the latest in the bridge beautification saga. They were at the last stoplight before reaching Abuelita's before Amalia gave into the temptation of glancing again at him.

"So." Amalia straightened his mostly-straight collar. "You clean up cute."

He flexed his bicep like she might be kidding. "Gotta look good for your granny."

"You turning into a flirt on me?"

He laughed like she hadn't been ogling him with intent. "I've learned a lot about communication thanks to you, but I have a long way to go before anyone could call me a flirt," he said.

"You're impossible," Amalia said, and decided not to clarify whether she meant good-impossible or hopeless-impossible. She didn't have much time to take a breath and recalibrate before they pulled up outside Abuelita's, but she gave it a shot. Nervy as it made her, she recognized that she'd been hot and cold with Dante. If she wanted more from him, she had to admit it, and act accordingly.

The house was already spilling over with family when they got there, plus half the neighborhood and more friends of friends than Amalia could keep track of.

They made their way through to the door, stopping for congratulations about the bridge project. About her FoundersFest Art Walk booth. About how lovely she looked on the arm of a handsome man.

Not that they were walking arm in arm. If she managed to work through the questions batting at her brain, though, maybe they would be by the time they left.

※≻≻≻♥≺≺≺※

The party was packed, chatter and laughs and music and a game of cards. He coasted along in Amalia's wake, charmed as hell to see her so relaxed and energized by all the chats and kisses and affectionate chaos.

"Drink?" he asked when she finally stopped circulating long enough to glance his way.

"Kitchen," she said with a wave in that direction. "Could you grab me a Topo Chico? I'll save you from my tíos."

The aromas hit before he was fully inside the room. Pots steamed, platters and bowls lined the counters, three women bustled around in one of those symphonies of coordination that suggested it wasn't their first time sharing a busy kitchen.

He recognized one of the aunts from the festival meeting. Not the one who'd thrust Amalia at him, but he held all the aunts in high regard on her account. "Anything I can do to help? Get things off a high shelf? Chop something?"

Cecily, the one whose name he knew, came in then, and shooed him away. "We've got a system, never you worry."

Drinks in hand, he searched out Amalia again, who'd ended up in the back yard under the tent.

As he approached, a voice rose over the crowd. "Dante Morales! Didn't I see you wearing that same shirt when you were buying Fern a beer?" It was his friend Steve, already halfway to laughing his ass off. That's when he remembered that Steve was on staff at Adrian Reyes's BBQ place. Amalia's brother was sitting beside the Steve, sending Dante a baleful look.

Dante dropped into a chair on the other side of Amalia, handing over her Topo Chico. "Only got the one dress shirt," he told Steve. He popped open his beer and leaned back, but Steve wasn't one to be deterred by an obvious sign to drop something.

"I guess you didn't get any of Fern's lipstick on your

collar, then. Or have you had time for laundry since Wednesday?"

"Fern and I had drinks on Tuesday. One drink." Wednesday was yoga day, not that Steve would know that. But he'd been planning to tell Amalia about Fern then, except Amalia hadn't shown up to class. And then, riding over to the party in her truck, he could smell her skin, and it distracted him out of being sensible.

"Yeah, well." Steve's smirk was irritating when they were in high school, and it wasn't any better now. "Maybe you were still wearing the shirt Wednesday morning for your walk of shame."

Dante helped himself to a handful of nuts from one of the bowls of snacks that sat on the little tables under the tent. "It's rude to speculate and gossip, man. And we didn't spend the night together. She's just a friend."

And then he busied himself with the boiled peanuts, cause he'd felt some spark between him and Amalia die out when Steve opened his mouth. Back before he and Amalia had started working together, Fern had turned down his offer to take her out. The morning after the flood, she'd called to say she'd heard about his working so hard for the town, and reconsidered. He'd been too exhausted and distracted by his workload to think through a better response, so he'd agreed. They'd set the date up for Tuesday and then he'd kinda forgotten, what with everything else. Amalia cooking for him. Amalia sleeping with him. Amalia propositioning him. Amalia coming under his hand and on his dick and in his mouth. Amalia making sweeping changes to the way Honey Wine saw its history.

He'd kept the date because, well. None of the lessons were about how to disappoint someone on purpose.

And instead, he'd gone and disappointed Amalia by mistake.

Dad and Tío Leon circulated through, warning people to go fill their plates so the tías could start setting out the second round of platters. Abuelita looked mighty proud of them for spending six minutes performing one sociable chore while her daughters and daughters-in-law had been cooking for the party for the better part of a week. As had Adrian, but slow-smoked brisket was his job.

Adrian gave her one of those brotherly looks when everyone else stood to get food, but she put a hand on Dante's arm to still him. She raised her brows at Adrian, who finally followed the crowd to the kitchen.

"Sounds like you've been busy," she said lightly. Like it was no big deal. Like hearing that he'd been dating Fern, of all people, wasn't five kinds of salt in her newly-diagnosed wound of him being perfectly fine with her push-pull attitude toward him.

Like Amalia wasn't being unfair as hell, minding his choices, when she hadn't made her own choices clear to him.

Jackson had mentioned seeing Dante at the bar on Tuesday. He hadn't mentioned Fern, which was unlike the head gossip of Town Square. If he'd been sparing her feelings, it seemed the rumors of those feelings were floating around before she'd managed to lock them up in her heart.

She didn't like how irked she was to find out it had been a date. Didn't like taking in the painfully clear answer it gave her to the question of what Dante wanted. Didn't like that it made her shoot barbed words at him. "If you had plans with your girlfriend you were free to cancel tonight."

His eyes flashed quick on hers. "Fern is not my girlfriend."

She couldn't read anything definite into his tone. Not disappointment. Not relief. Just facts. She tried to give him back an equal amount of indifference, though she could tell that even her one-syllable reply was shaky with suppressed hope. "Oh."

"Amalia," he said, gentle, like he wasn't sure what else he could say.

"It's fine." She hoped her smile wasn't tight enough to look forced. "Congrats to us both for everything we've accomplished since we started this whole thing, I guess."

She kind of hated herself for being exactly as impossible as she'd accused him of being. She was starting to fear that the better Dante got at becoming someone's ideal match, the worse she herself was getting at processing and understanding her emotions.

Before she could burn any more of whatever goodwill he still had for her to the ground, she headed inside to fill herself with tacos.

CHAPTER 23

He sat there for a while, swirling his beer and trying not to focus too hard on watching the door Amalia had walked through. Even tried chatting with Adrian when he came back with more food than any one person could possibly eat, but he wasn't sure if the awkward small talk they attempted was worse or better than the awkward silence that followed it.

Eventually, he wandered off to make himself marginally useful. Hauled some chairs out from inside so older folks could sit under the shade. Sorted out which dishes were gluten-free for some couple who looked confused by the array of tortillas. Carted dirty plates in from the yard. And, mostly, managed to avoid being trapped into more uncomfortable conversations.

He didn't manage to avoid his circling thoughts about why the hell he was still there. He could have caught a ride with someone; he could have walked; he could have called Johnny to come get him when he finished the quick call-out Dante had dispatched him on. Hell, he could have called Johnny to pick him up right away and pretended the guy needed help retrieving a ring from a P-trap.

Communication and fucking honesty, though.

So he ought to be more patient. With himself, for sure. With Amalia, too. The Fern news had come as a surprise to her, and he'd been at fault. He ought to have told her. Or canceled it, what with his intense feelings about Amalia getting even worse once they'd slept together. It'd been a dick move to keep the date when he was hung up on someone else, but some part of him—*probably* not the same part that was hurt at how Amalia had withdrawn since their night in his bed, though there would be a Venn diagram overlap—was thinking he should test himself with someone else. See if his thing for Amalia was entirely for her, or if he'd fixed his attention on her just cause she was the one there when he'd sliced himself open. If maybe his feelings were just the basic relief of hanging out with a woman who understood what a needy and shoddy lover he was.

Or maybe not shoddy anymore, if that night was any evidence. And it had to count for something, at least in terms of his sex skills. Amalia would have told him if he had failed her in bed.

That was also kind of the problem, though. She'd have told him if he had succeeded in any relationship-type ways. And she hadn't made any effort to do that, not even in her usual matter-of-fact style.

He knew it wasn't wise of him to equate zero complaints from her with a deluge of compliments. He'd gotten all flustered when she'd called him cute on the way to the party, and he hadn't known what to do with that.

So he set out to clean up the kitchen, sending the bevy of aunts out to spend some time with their relatives. The way they protested, but clearly wanted the freedom to enjoy the party, gave him pause. Gave him a stark reality check about the familial environment she lived in.

Amalia was so determined to put her career and artistic

goals first. No one should have to back-burner their passions, but seeing her family in action really clarified why she was so staunch about it.

Eventually the leftovers were packed away and the borrowed chairs were sorted by style to make it easier for everyone to reclaim their own, and parents had collected their drowsy children.

Eventually he and Amalia headed back to her truck.

"Thanks for helping out so much."

He shrugged, and then recalled how he wanted to not shrug off communication with her. Not when there could be a thrilling alternative. "Happy to help."

She pulled out of her grandmother's street. "I guess. Anyway, you have a house of fans there now."

"Except for your brother. And, it seems, except for you?"

She let out a sharp breath that might also have been a small laugh. They sat in silence for a bit. Let the cab of the truck fill with road noises and the almost meditative rhythm of streetlights dotting light onto the world outside.

He needed to crack open what was solidifying around them.

"Can we—maybe you can pull over somewhere?"

She glanced at him. Back at the road. "We'll be at your place in eight minutes."

"I know." He could talk at her for all eight minutes, but his sense was it'd be wiser to make the setting more interactive. More personal.

She sighed, but she also pulled over and parked in a burger stand's parking lot. The ticking of the quiet night surrounded them.

"Thanks." He took in one long breath. "I'm sorry about Fern. I should have told you."

She sat very still, her hands loose on the wheel like she didn't care not to have something to hold onto. "You didn't owe me anything."

"Not true," he said, and watched her expression change. Lighten. "And not just because the date happened after you and I—"

Her fingers flexed. He took it as encouragement to go on.

"I'll tell you what I was thinking, because I want to be clear, but it's not excusing myself, okay? She called right after the date with Natasha, and since that didn't work out —even without the flood it wasn't going to work out—I was thinking I should try again, without the supervision, to see if it made a difference. But that wasn't even a ... a full thought, I guess. I was tired. I put it on my calendar and went back to drain maintenance. I know that doesn't matter, in the end, cause I still went, but I do want you knowing I didn't seek her out after you and I ... after we were together."

She nodded, still staring at the dark restaurant windows.

"A big part of me was scared we, you and me, were done. When you didn't talk to me after the meeting, didn't even go to yoga, that felt rough. Like we didn't even have friendship anymore. And when it came to it, yeah, I was curious what it would be like to be on a proper real date with someone. One we set up just because it was what we wanted, cause she picked me, and not because of our scheme. But I should have told you. And I shouldn't have gone. I could feel as soon as I got there that I was wrong for not canceling."

"You're free to date who you like." She sounded like she was gritting out the words.

"Fucking hell, Amalia. I'm not interested in dating Fern, or anyone else for that matter."

That got her looking at him at last. "You can be interested in whoever you want."

"True. And I'd like to be interested in you. I already am interested in you. Have been, for a long time now." He adored how her face softened a bit. He went deeper into it. "If you're interested back, I'd like that a lot."

It seemed past time for her to stop setting up barriers. Her thoughts and her heartbeat were both racing like nonsense, so it was a good thing he'd asked her to pull over. "Right," she said, while she figured out where to start. "So, maybe you missed it, but I was flirting with you today."

He looked as stunned as if she had called him honey-pie. As if she'd withheld so much affection from him that one blunt statement walloped him. It hurt almost as bad as hearing him say how much she'd left him feeling unchosen. "When?"

"On the way to the party," she admitted. "I said you were cute."

"Huh." He went thoughtful for a second too long. "And I joked it off, and then you found out about Fern."

"It's been a hell of a night." She sounded bitter to her own ears, and that didn't feel justified. It was something she needed to unpack. She had to stop thinking in terms of keeping accounts, and start admitting to having complex, intense emotions. "I get it, though. I was thrown, but—"

"I should have—"

She cut him off, turning as fully to face him as her seat belt allowed, and planting her palm on his knee.

"I want you knowing I like you, too. Since my flirting didn't make that clear," she said, and the bitterness was gone entirely. Touching him was closing an open circuit inside her. "I've been letting myself stay too busy to think about it, which wasn't fair to either of us. And I didn't realize how much I wasn't coming clean—to either of us—until I got hit by jealousy about Fern. That was not fun."

"Good," he said, and his smile looked like relief. "Not good that it wasn't fun, but—"

"I know. And thanks for telling me about what it was like

when I left you in the cold. That was uncalled for, and I shouldn't have." It left the worst taste in her mouth, thinking about how he would have sunk into that insecurity. "I focused on work. I mean, I had to do the work, but not to the point that I couldn't have called you."

"Hey. I saw how things were tonight, with your family. With the women in your family. I'd never ask you to put your goals in the back seat, Amalia. I admire your goals, in case that's not clear by now, and even when they take you away from here, I'm still going to be so excited for you."

Her heart and mind were playing ping-pong with her attention, but that just didn't make sense. "What do you mean, when they take me away?"

"Wherever your art takes you. To cities to put in installations or museums to curate shows or whatever it is artists on your level do to grow to even higher levels. Like I told Mike, you're too good for Honey Wine."

"Dante." She shook her head. He'd been thinking things like that all along? "Honey Wine is where my family is. My community, my friends. This is *home*. You think I set up my studio and workshop where I did on a whim? I want to be here, I want to be around when my granny or parents need help, and to baby the little cousins, and to remind my brother that when *Texas Monthly* wrote up his place, they said, and I quote, 'Pitmaster Reyes is the brother of noted Texas sculptor Amalia Reyes.' Maybe I'll get opportunities to travel, and that's nice, but I'll always come back here."

"Yeah?"

"Yeah. Absolutely yeah."

"In that case. If you mean it about liking me. If that means we can be in a relationship—?"

"Yep. Please, yes."

Even in the dark of the parking lot, he glowed at her. "Good. But, Amalia, please don't ice me out like that again. I don't have an issue with your work coming first, but you shouldn't use it as an excuse to ignore me. Honesty and communication, right?"

She thunked her head against the steering wheel, mostly for effect. "Do I have to say how our deal has taught me a thing or two, or can I just prove I've learned the lesson by doing better in the future?"

He linked their fingers together. "If you're talking about a future with me, I'm pretty much too happy right now to make demands."

Her grin likely eclipsed his. She released her seatbelt, and then, when he reached for his own, covered his hand with hers.

It was a little sneaky, and a lot fun, to leave him strapped in while she leaned over. Whispered into the air between them, "I know you can sit still for me. You're so, so strong at staying still for me."

It meant she had to half climb over the console, but his reaction made it worth any discomfort. He made a low sound that filled her ears, and sparked vibrations through her entire body, as his head tipped to meet hers. His mouth opened under her eager kiss, both gusting relieved breaths.

Inelegance and awkwardness and everything perfect. She let one of her hands tangle in his hair while he cupped the side of her neck, and it was tender enough to send bright hope crashing all through her.

The urgency was still there when they broke away, but something else hovered between them, too. Delight, maybe, or the simplicity of potential. It made her breathless in a different—and equally welcome—way.

"Amalia," he said, slow in that molasses way she relished, "You've got to know how much I adore you."

She sank back into her seat, dropping her head against the rest. She laid her palm on the console and he interlaced their fingers. They both squeezed, and Amalia nodded. And nodded again, since things were going so well.

"And since the feeling's mutual ... Seven minutes to get back to your place. Or I can take the next right and it'll be five minutes to mine. Thoughts?"

"Take the right."

CHAPTER 24

They didn't make it to the bed.

The click of the door unlocking was probably some kind of permanent turn-on now. Shoes off as they kissed against the wall. His fingers under her shirt, hers working his buttons. Pressing close as they ran lips and hands all over each other. Stumble-kissing, stumble-groping, stumble-laughing, and then he tumbled into that green armchair that always welcomed him into her home.

His pulled her into his lap, straddling his legs, and he was suddenly aware of how far things had already gone. Her shirt rode up, just below her breasts, and when his fingers brushed her abs, he paused.

"Hi," he said, before kissing her throat.

"Hi to you."

"This okay? Need to give me notes?"

She shoved the panels of his shirt aside and raked her blunt nails up his chest. "No worries, star student. We are so good."

He hummed agreement and got her shirt over her head. He trailed more kissed down the center of her chest, and her breathing got rapid and she held him tight to him, and his cock got harder. And he was so fucking proud to be holding her back. To be turning her on.

He traced the triangle cups of her bra with one rough finger, dropping slow, intermittent kisses on her shoulders and arms and cheeks.

He let his other hand float to her hip, her back, the band of her skirt. He collected all her gasps and trapped them in his heart.

"I'm getting impatient here, Dante. How's that for irony? Can we get on with it?"

"It?"

She rocked forward, laughing at his own gasps. He strained towards her, agony and eagerness and joy. Together they half-slid to the floor, landing on one of those plush rugs of hers, and skimmed off his pants and her skirt.

As soon as he was horizontal, she straddled him. He released her hair clip and fanned all that loveliness out to enclose them in a cave of their own making. Kissed her hard, but only teased her with his tongue.

She was liquid fire against him—all hot skin against skin—and when he melted into the floor with her lovely weight atop him, Dante was hit with a blast of clarity.

"It's not validation," he said.

She arched up some to look down at him. "Good to know?"

"Don't get me wrong, I do love it. Feeling desired. Could be my self-image stuff will always plague me to some extent. But I worked through it, and that's not the reason I want a partner."

Amalia sat up fully and shifted so she was leaning against the couch.

He did the same, and never mind how they were both in just their underwear. He told her the rest of his answer as to why he was looking for a relationship. "I was scared my reasons were what you said, about having a trophy to show off my own worthiness. And like I said, it's helpful for a part of me to feel like I'm attractive enough—"

"You're a stud and you know it."

"Don't start complimenting me, Amalia, I can't take it. Well, I can, but not just this minute. Besides, I mean attractive on the inside. You're this amazing bright talented—and gorgeous—woman, and I'm having trouble trusting you're not too good for me. Which is my problem to subdue."

She grabbed his thigh, real close to his hip, and shook the muscle like she wanted to rearrange his atoms.

He laughed, and then she laughed, and the thing about laughing while nearly nude was what a delight it was to see her stomach muscles rippling with her glee.

He bit his lip until he could speak clearly again. "Shared pleasure. That's the thing I want. I want to take pleasure in being with you, and for you to take pleasure in being with me. For us to connect over the things we like, and to have fun appreciating that the other likes whatever weird things they're into."

"I'm not putting pickle juice in my soda. Stop asking."

He kissed her and she straddled his lap again. He linked his arms behind the small of her back. "I might put a jar of pickles in your fridge at some point, but I'd never ask you to consume them."

"We can manage that."

"Yeah?"

"Yeah, of course. Can we fuck now? You're making me wild with all this cute stud energy."

He scooped her up as he stood, and took her to her bed.

⇢⤏⤏⤏♥⤎⤎⤎⇠

She hooked her fingers in the waistband of his boxers and got them halfway down his thighs before he had to do the rest. Then she shoved him to lie flat while she wriggled out of her own underwear. He groaned, pulling her over him like a favorite blanket. They rolled, and she wrapped her legs around him, holding him tight, cause it seemed like they were both determined to maintain as much contact as possible.

He managed to kiss so many new places. The inside of her elbow. The underside of her breast. The shell of her ear. She'd thought they'd explored each other all over, but the brush of his beard on tender skin proved that was a lie. Amalia was breaking into goosebumps, and the shivery goodness made her wetter.

"Condom," she demanded, while she still had breath to do so.

"Yeah, yes." He rolled it on, then moved down the length of her body until her knees were wide and he was breathing harsh and eager above her. And then Dante filled her slowly, steadily, a look of reverence on his face as he watched hers.

"Fuck," she said, because it was right, and it was true, and it was fucking perfect to have him thrusting hard and fast for a few seconds before bringing his mouth down on hers again. He'd remembered exactly how to stroke her clit. He balanced on one elbow while his opposite hand worked between them, and every few thrusts he kissed her cheeks, her eyes, her neck, her lips.

Amalia was leaving bruises on his shoulders, she was gripping him so hard as she pressed her own thrusts up to meet his. Dante touched his lips to her fingers and caught his breath when she clamped her muscles around him. His groan, desperate and low, got downright growly when she gripped his wrist and convulsed around him. It was hard to say his whole name, with her breath sawing out of her, so she chanted, "Dant, Dant, Dant," through her shocks and aftershocks.

He was right there with her. Of course he was. He buried his head in the crook of her neck, groaning and shaking through a frenzy of thrusts, and when he dropped on top of her, she could feel his heart pounding as strong as she could feel her own.

Another tender kiss, once they were breathing more normally, before they unstuck to lay side by side. She kept tracing his upper arm with her blunt nails, and he kept smiling at her from his pillow. Deep satisfaction and languor warmed her even before Dante returned from the bathroom with glasses of water and tidied the bedding over them.

"I noticed something," she said as they snuggled in.

"Was it my dick? I meant you to see that."

"Funny. That's not the something I meant." She ran her thumb over a wet spot on his lip.

He set aside his glass. "Then what?"

"When you told me what you realized you wanted, there was something about the way you said it."

Dante closed his eyes, either re-running his memory of his words or ineffectually hiding from them. "Go on. Put me out of my misery."

"Do you know you went from saying 'a relationship' to talking about me, specifically, that you want to share pleasure with?"

He must have heard the smile in her voice, since he was reaching for her hand before he even opened his eyes. "I didn't notice, no. Huh."

"Huh, indeed. You started out all neutral, but then it was all pickle jars in my fridge."

"I don't actually like pickles all that much. Sorry to ruin the mystique."

"Get out of my bed." But she said it deadpan and tightened her hold on his hand. He rolled closer for a deep kiss.

When they were laying face to face, Dante said, "I worked out the desire stuff when I never thought I had a chance with you. I'm sure every relationship has its own values and strengths, but at this stage in my life, the reasons I was looking for a partner probably hold even if that partner isn't you. It's just that, somewhere along the way when I was figuring all that out, I fell in love with you, so. Yeah. It's you, specifically, Amalia, who I want to share pleasure with."

And there went her heart, bursting into flames and rising from the ashes and bursting into flames again.

She didn't give him a chance to backtrack or equivocate or bury his head under a pillow. She got the words out, decisive and sure, because she never, ever, wanted him to question it. "I fell in love with you, too."

EPILOGUE

Dante maneuvered through the throngs strolling the Art Walk as they made their way to and from the music stage and food tents. Someone else was keeping official attendance, but that hadn't stopped Jackson Apel from regaling him with his own estimates, and his opinions about it being a cheerier crowd than in the past, and his comparison of this year's weather with that of every final weekend of July during the previous decade.

He stopped to deliver a bag of pastries to Nicole's booth. He'd offered up Leo as her assistant for the festival, and his cousin seemed to have managed to direct his energies towards working the crowd and hawking her prints. Dante hadn't expected Leo's brother to be far off, but he was surprised to spot Enrique on a bean bag chair at the back of the booth, with Nicole's kid climbing over him demanding he read another book. Dante went brows-up at Leo, who shook his head and mimed a swoon.

He'd be following up on *that* later.

As he approached Amalia's booth, her dad was talking up the bridge project to a group waiting their turn to take selfies in front of Amalia's Apple Mill Bridge installation. Back in June, he'd first asked how he and her mom could help, and then offered to be her brand ambassadors, and by the end of the month had insisted she approve a flyer he wanted to hand out to festival-goers explaining the art.

She'd acted for a moment like her parents' vocal support was embarrassing, until Tía Cecily told her they were allowed to be proud of their talented daughter, and then Dante'd handed over a handkerchief before she could even pretend she wasn't tearing up. And then Abuelita fussed over how thoughtful Dante was, and Amalia rolled her eyes, and Adrian made kissy noises, and ... yeah. Things with her family were feeling less contentious.

Not contentious at all: how Amalia's was the most dynamic and crowd-stopping of the bridge art installations. It wasn't only his opinion. Livia said she'd heard the same sentiment from her B&B guests, and Amalia's had the most hashtags when he searched, and collectors kept dropping by her booth to mention the galleries they worked with.

Dante set her kolaches and smoothie on her work table. He moved to the front of the booth to take over talking for a bit, so Amalia could have a break. "Thanks, love."

He bent for her kiss. "Anytime. Get some shade."

Amalia ducked out of the sun, but kept within earshot in case she had to elaborate on something. As if he hadn't memorized the info he needed to explain to a customer, "Good eye, yeah—this piece is part of the next evolution of Amalia's rasquache period. See how she picks up the feeling of the Blanco River running over the cypress trees? You'll see it's an echo of the left side of the bridge art."

When he backed off to let them browse, he caught sight of Mr. Connor rounding the corner. Amalia was finishing up her pastry, so Mr. Connor stopped to chat with Dante.

"Busy day, huh?" Mr. Connor's eyes crinkled with pleasure.

"A good turnout, yeah."

"I'd say our best yet." He turned toward Amalia, who

brushed off sugar crumbs as she joined them. "Two things, Amalia. First, the council wants to buy the Apple Mill Bridge piece and have you make it a permanent feature of the bridge once construction is through."

Her eyes got wide. She wrapped an arm around Dante's waist and squeezed. He kissed the top of her head. "You're amazing, that's excellent."

"I am, right?" She grinned. "Thanks."

"You are welcome, but neither the praise nor the purchase are meant to influence your decision on my second point. The FoundersFest committee is asking if you'll take over the Art Walk subcommittee for next year. They've decided that as we grow in size and ..." Mr. Connor looked around for eavesdroppers, "and scope, that the workload is no longer suited to Mike Moll's particular skill set."

Dante turned his head to the back of the tent and clamped his mouth shut to keep from barking out a laugh. Amalia's shoulders shook under his arm.

Mr. Connor nodded. "We won't need an immediate answer, but planning for next year begins with the postmortem on this year, while it's fresh in everyone's minds. So, check your email when you've rested up from the weekend, and let us know."

She promised she would, and they waited until Mr. Connor was out of sight before retreating to the shadows and propping each other up, laughing loud enough to drown out the nearby polka band.

Their town had—as was right—welcomed Amalia's ideas with open arms, and his part in facilitating that would always be gratifying. Not as gratifying as sleeping every night with the woman he loved, but Dante made room in his life for joys of all sizes. And there was nothing as joyful as sharing his life with the petite, huge spirited, loving and caring Amalia Reyes.

Thank you for reading STILL WATERS. I hope you've had fun diving into the world of Amalia, Dante, and Honey Wine.

If you'd like to see how the Hearts of Honey Wine series began, keep reading for Chapter One of COMMON GROUND.

As you know, honest feedback helps other readers find new books. Please take a moment to review STILL WATERS at some of the top retailers / review sites.

Amazon / Goodreads / BookBub / Other Retailers

COMMON GROUND, CHAPTER 1

"Y'all, I'm telling you, you've never heard such quiet." Livia Delacroix aimed her camera through the slightly wavy glass front door of Chata Bed and Breakfast. She'd signed away most of her inheritance to buy the small hotel, sure her mom would have approved of Livia making it the business of her dreams.

Almost entirely sure. Sure enough to make up for any smidges of anxiety that she was in over her head, relocating to the town she hadn't even seen since she was thirteen.

So it was okay if her first impressions of Chata were … lonelier than she'd hoped. Outside, there was nothing but dusk and—well, nothing. Dusky sky, undulating dark line of trees, hills and fields impossible to see.

She kept her narration upbeat as she moved up the stairs. Probably she'd edit it out. Overlay a more sensible audio when she put the video together. Her friend Maggie had advised her to talk through this first gander of her new venture. Her initial reactions could be gold. Livia hid all her doubts, and kept talking. "I know what you're thinking: how do you hear quiet, right? But I bet you know what I mean. It's nothing but crickets and owls out here. Are they crickets, do you suppose? Grasshoppers? Frogs? What chirps at night?"

Maggie would be snorting about now if she heard this footage. Livia grinned, pausing at the first guest room door. "My intuition says they're crickets. So I'm sticking with that. And if it turns out the charming little town of Honey Wine, Texas, is overtaken with marauding locusts, y'all can laugh at me later. Okay. This first room is called Persimmon."

She switched on the overhead light and gasped. Remembered to keep her camera steady and her dismay curtailed.

Livia had expected some surprises, sure. She'd bought the place sight unseen, with only outdated website photos, vague memories of a brief stay with her mom, and a good report from her structural engineer as evidence that she hadn't lost her hard-won good sense.

Not that she'd been slip-shod about the process. Kent Stipple, the former owner, wanted to sell fast without involving realtors; he'd grumbled that there was nothing they could do he couldn't manage himself. Chata B&B had been his wife Sissy's passion, but she'd died over a year earlier, and he was ready to retire. Livia had talked to him about everything Chata—which translated to "cottage" in Czech. How cute was that? A sweet nod to the Bohemians that had settled the Hill County town of Honey Wine back in the mid-1800s.

Before closing, she'd gone over the accounts with a fine-tooth comb and reviewed every report. She knew that she'd find that Chata was as much rough as diamond. But she'd signed the papers, rented a trailer, and now stood in the middle of Persimmon, ready to concede that she might not have been entirely prepared for this undertaking.

She was tempted to call Mags and brainstorm solutions that would let her back out of this venture unscathed. Only the thought of her friend's sardonic comments kept her from outright fleeing.

The building itself had all the rustic charm she'd remembered. Good bones. The common areas were slightly worn, but the kitchen was large, with gracious windows overlooking the ranks of trees. The high end appliances, only a few years old, circled a large central island.

Every time she explained how Chata was everything she'd always dreamed of, Maggie and other friends from their hotel management program found increasingly less polite ways to call her a fool. Sure, Livia had entertained secret doubts, even while working through her never-ending 'before I move' checklist. But she'd ridden up the uneven, unpaved drive to the building, just as twilight settled the surrounding hills into dusky tranquility, and felt peace descend.

All traces of that peace fled when she walked into Persimmon.

"Right. Well. The layout isn't bad. We have a spacious king bed, daybed tucked against the wall, this great brick and tile fireplace. Desk and two—oh."

Her attempts to cheerfully narrate the video skittered south.

"Yeah, so this will not be in the final cut. Do you see how that armchair's missing half its fabric down the side? Do you see how it clashes with the wallpaper?" She laughed shortly. "Not that I'm likely to keep that up. Top of the list of things to replace, honestly. Or top, so far."

She trailed off as she spotted ragged holes in the foam under the frayed fabric of the armchair. Not obviously made by animals, but if critters were the culprit, she wouldn't be surprised. Spinning slowly, she took in the room. It was a good size. The window and doors were sturdy. She couldn't smell mold or mildew. In fact, the B&B's air was pleasant, thanks to the cedar or cypress or whatever other fragrant trees that covered the property.

She could work with it.

She had to. She'd sunk every one of her options into it.

Boosting a smile into her voice, she said, "I love Persimmon. It is unique. One of a kind." Or so she hoped. She still had to investigate Chickasaw, Mulberry, Loquat, and Jujube.

She undercut her entire point by focusing in on the fireplace mantle, where five angels perched. They were all different styles—ceramic, plaster, something that might be cornhusk.

And then she zoomed in on the four mismatched lamps. The angular brass 70s-era one by the porch door. On the desk, a porcelain urn-shaped base with celadon glaze and a gilt-rimmed inset of a pastoral French scene. The one on the left bedside table, with a scrolled plaster of Paris base topped with a bust.

"I think that's Mozart," she told her camera, of the bewigged man with a flouncy shirt and a violin resting against his chest. "Could be Brahms? Not Beethoven, though. I'd recognize him for sure. Shame I can't read music, because whoever's symphony is decoupaged on the shade might give me a hint."

She was going to have to cut so much wobbly camera work when she edited this video. Livia barely had her shaking shoulders under control by the time she'd circled to the other bedside table. And then she lost it again.

In the ill-lit photos on the website, Persimmon had seemed full of wood and charming rag rugs and comfortably upholstered furniture. She couldn't begin to remember what the lamps had looked like. But definitely not like this.

She'd have remembered this.

The final lamp base was boldly painted resin of a cowboy astride his horse, and the dangling light switch was his lasso. She managed a close-up of his seen-too-much, far-reaching gaze, before shutting off the recording and collapsing on the mercifully comfortable bed.

She took a quick photo to text to Maggie, because she needed to share the hilarity. Needed to have at least some sense of not being completely alone as she explored her new home and business. It might get creepy otherwise, all this darkness, and the chirping bugs, and the boards that creaked underfoot.

And if she felt totally alone, she might start wondering what she'd gotten herself into.

Buying Chata sight unseen hadn't seemed that wild a plan. Sure, when she'd made the offer, Mags and the others had mentioned that most people didn't blow their inheritance on some property hundreds of miles from any place they'd ever lived, even with all her research about the town's growing tourism economy. Didn't go from managing the high thread-count luxury of a European-style Dallas hotel to sole proprietorship of a five-room B&B on the outskirts of a small Hill Country town. No matter how quaint it looked on the website. No matter her sepia-tinged memories of that one spring break getaway she and Mom had spent at Chata. Or the remembered comfort of the safe haven Mom had tried to create for the two of them post-divorce, back before they'd locked horns in an unresolved clash, followed by Livia's impetuous flouncing away.

Her mom, the one of comfort and support, would have wanted Livia to pursue her dreams. And if she caught herself rubbing her thumb over the contours of Mom's old ruby ring on her right hand at the thought, that was just a habit. It meant nothing.

She pretended that if she said it enough, she wouldn't be making it up. Pretended that she knew what her mom would have thought about her wild venture. Pretended that Mags didn't know damn good and well that Livia was pretending.

Prior to discovering Chata, Livia would have said things were fine. No, she and Mom hadn't been close since before Livia left for college, but they talked a few times a year. Mom consistently said how much she just wanted Livia to be happy, even if she never seemed to grasp the difference between the unsophisticated, resentful suburban girl Livia had been at seventeen and the well-traveled, competent hotelier she'd become.

So after Mom's death, she'd gone on with life as usual. Well, life as usual, if her usual life hadn't been contaminated by those five long years with Terry, and also, somewhere in the sub-structure, the festering disconnect from her mom. Really, what went on as usual was work. Always work.

And then she'd covered someone's shift and wound up stuck on front desk duty one slow evening, with little to distract her from idle thoughts of the directionless expanse of her future.

And Livia preferred not to think about the directionless expanse of her future.

Between occasional calls from guests, she'd read an industry magazine cover to cover, and ran across Kent's ad. "For Sale: rustic B&B in scenic Honey Wine. Newly updated, regular occupancy, make Chata's past a part of your future." The black-and-white photo showed a wood-frame three-story house with porches wrapping each level, absolutely surrounded by trees and empty sky.

Livia's heart had unaccountably leapt when she'd seen it. It took a good few minutes of staring, hand to her chest, before she reconciled it with that half-buried memory of her and Mom eating pie at a diner, plunging into a deep blue swimming hole along the river, and reading on a porch while hummingbirds darted overhead.

By the time her shift was over, she'd read every review of Chata B&B on three travel sites, half-memorized the layout of Honey Wine from the town's tourism page, and surreptitiously logged in to her bank account so she could stare, again, some more, at the balance that had landed there after probate on her mom's will was cleared.

The next morning, she'd phoned Kent.

Chata was still there. Still for sale. She could afford it.

Within a couple of weeks, they'd worked out a deal. Within a couple of months, the deal had closed.

She'd kept meaning to take some time off, to make the five-hour drive to see it again in person, but giving notice to the hotel had sent the owners into crisis mode. They'd recruited her straight out of college and shepherded her to her current position; it had been the definitive move she'd needed to make to escape Terry's cycles of control. Livia wanted to leave things in experienced hands. Which meant interviewing. And more interviewing. And then hiring, and training, and more training. By the time they'd squared everything away, it was her closing date, so she checked her gut, found she was still inordinately excited about Chata, and signed the papers.

It was almost weirder that she never met Kent than it was that she hadn't seen Chata in fifteen years. They'd used different branches of the same title company. She'd hired a local inspector and surveyor to check the place out, and he'd sent his books to her once they'd signed the sales contract. All in all, Livia was pretty impressed with how honestly the old guy had represented his property. Everything he'd said—that the bathrooms were outdated but functional, and the driveway uneven, but the well water was pure and the kitchen was commercial quality—checked out. For all his hard-to-understand mumble-grumble over the phone lines, and his distrust of realtors that had led him to place the sales ad, Kent had kept the place in good repair and, most importantly, kept heads on beds. Repeat heads on beds, actually—there were folks on the review sites that mentioned they returned to Honey Wine every couple of years, and always stayed at Chata.

It boded well. And what Livia really, deeply, desperately wanted in her life was something that boded well.

She wasn't a fool. Her friends said it was nothing but magical thinking, when she'd been careless enough to tell them that Chata just felt right, but there was more to it than what they termed her "run away to the country and pretend that the simple life's the life for you" philosophy. First off, she wasn't running. She'd always planned on owning her own place someday, from the moment she'd enrolled in the hospitality program. And she'd done damn well in school—damn well at her job, too. All of it in service of her dream—to have business cards reading "Livia DeLacroix, Owner."

And now she could.

If it also meant she could leave behind some bad memories and a handful of the less charming aspects of Dallas, that was nothing but a bonus.

After the shocks of Persimmon, she gave up on attempting to record her initial impressions of Chata, stowing her phone while she explored the rest of the rooms. They were definitely … singular. She'd examine closer in the light of day, but most of what she clocked seemed, as expected, cosmetic. Kent had included all furnishings and decor with the deal, other than the stuff in the top floor owner's suite.

Livia had a few furnishings of her own in the trailer—her comfortable desk chair, the dinette set from her apartment, a storage chest she'd mostly packed because it had been with her so long it was hard to imagine a new life without it. The few of her mom's stained-glass windows that survived after cleaning out her house. But mostly she'd brought clothes, books, electronics, and her stack of pillows and bedding. She carted a few armloads up to the owner's suite before returning to Persimmon, and settling down against the rickety brass headboard to make notes by the light of the atrocious lamps.

It ought to have been enough to exhaust her into sleep, even with the strange surroundings. But her mind leapt in chaotic rhythm, cataloging the night sounds—surely those were crickets—and flashing on odd new worries. Would her wifi be strong in all the guest rooms? What if her guests were used to some unknown favorite breakfast treat of Kent's and resented her famous jalapeño cornbread muffins? What would she find to replace the collection of scary angels on Persimmon's mantle?

After a half-restful night, Livia started early the next morning, unloading the trailer all by her lonesome. So Maggie could just bite her skeptical tongue. Never mind that she left the table and half her boxes stacked in the entryway for the time being. Livia needed to return the trailer and deal with her own transportation needs before she could do much of anything else.

She followed all the twists and turns to the interstate and zipped up to a nearby town where she could finally unhitch. Of course, if she'd realized how difficult the road up to Chata would be on her sedan's suspension, she could have skipped installing a trailer hitch on it and bought something sturdier to begin with. But never mind. She searched for used car dealers while waiting on the rental trailer paperwork, glad she'd kept easy access to her car's title while organizing herself for the big move. It took the expected bit of negotiation, but by the time Livia stopped by a grocery store to stock up, she was in her brand new, pale blue, slightly used pickup. Bonnie, she named it, short for the state flower, bluebonnets, which carpeted the Hill Country every spring.

The salesperson took a picture of her sitting in the truck's cab, which she sent to the Dallas group text before heading back to Chata.

Back home.

Livia was pretty darn proud of herself.

Even if no one else was around to hear her brag about it.

By the middle of her third morning at Chata, Livia was dying for someone to brag to. Not for the sake of the bragging —though her lists were kick-ass levels of thoroughness—but because the crickets and deer and the corpses of dried out millipedes filling one corner of Bonnie's garage were all the company she'd had, and it would have been nice to see a familiar face. Or even an unfamiliar one.

Too bad she'd had Kent block off bookings for several weeks so she could renovate and settle in.

Mags pointed out, during one of the calls Livia was initiating too often, that if Livia could go through the entire process of buying Chata without driving down to see the place, she shouldn't already be begging her friends to visit.

"But you'll love these hills," Livia wheedled. "You should see how purple and azure the sky is as the sun sets over the treetops. And watching the stars come out! It's like nothing you'd ever see in Dallas. You know you'd enjoy that."

"Yep, one day. I have my doubts about your motives just now."

"Some friend."

"Live with it. Now go away. I know you keep calling so I'll get fired for personal calls at work and not have that as an excuse to stay put."

She snickered, as her friend must have intended. "You saw through my diabolical plan?"

"I'm clever that way. Go make a grocery list or something. I sent the crumb cake recipe, by the way. Check your email."

"You're the best."

"Damn straight. Don't forget it."

"Love you, Mags."

"Yeah, yeah. Later." Maggie hung up.

Livia carried her third cup of morning coffee up to her top floor suite. She'd begun moving some of the weirder—but still in decent shape—furniture up to her own space, giving her more latitude to rearrange and redecorate the guest rooms. She was measuring for new blinds when a cloud of dust down the hill caught her attention. It grew closer. By the time Livia moved to the window with the best view, she'd discounted a pile of possibilities. The satellite internet guys weren't due for three more days. The mailman left everything down by the street. Kent had called from Louisiana the previous day to report that he'd gotten a royal flush at the poker tables. Though why he'd thought Livia needed to know that, she wasn't sure. Maybe he wanted to give her an opening in case she needed to yell about the millipedes.

So she wasn't expecting anything to be climbing up her rocky driveway. She checked her cell phone was getting a signal and ducked back into the shadows, hoping to see without being seen. A dusty SUV swung into the parking area, barely missing Bonnie, and the silence once it was off was as loud as had been the noise of it trekking up the hill.

Livia stood back and watched as an athletic, tall, dark, and possibly handsome—under his ball cap it was hard to tell—stranger emerged and turned to stare, balefully, straight up at her top-floor window.

ACKNOWLEDGMENTS

Friends! As you guessed from reading it, I feel so tenderly towards Dante and Amalia. They've been (mostly) a pleasure to bring to the page, and I (mostly) couldn't have done it without all kinds of support. (One of you *pretends* to be supportive while actually trolling me all the time; you know who you are.) (I like you just the way you are.)

My Greene Team, who help get the word out about all my new releases—thank you for being a vital part of my authorial journey. (If you'd like to join, sign up here.)

My invaluable, insightful editor Jen Prokop, and kind sensitivity reader Melissa of Salt & Sage Books (all mistakes mine, of course!), and the wise Sarah MacLean and my cohort from her conflict class, who helped me brainstorm this sex deal—all of you made this book stronger, and I hope it shows in big and intimate ways.

Magnificent Firebirds! I bet you picked up on some in-jokes. Yes, I meant for all of them to make you smile. Thanks for being a welcoming place to hang out and talk all things romance in such fun, smart, inspiring, and bananas ways.

I dedicated this book to my parents because when I wanted to learn to write fiction, they gave me a desk and a typewriter. And when I wanted to learn to weld, they took me to their workshop and handed me their face mask and gloves. Those events were four decades apart, so you can imagine how full my life has been of moments of support and encouragement.

Speaking of encouragement: Robert, David, and Kieran. You three are everything. 🤍

ABOUT THE AUTHOR

Melanie Greene lives in a tiny woodland cottage in a big skyscraper city, with her husband and kids and pets and plants and all the people inhabiting her imagination.

For more info, visit her at www.melaniegreene.com, where you can also sign up for her newsletter to access new releases and bonus content.

- instagram.com/melaniegreeneauthor
- bsky.app/profile/melaniegreene.bsky.social
- bookbub.com/authors/melanie-greene

Made in the USA
Columbia, SC
28 June 2025